D0189833

SUPERNATURAL

BOBBY SINGER'S
GUIDE TO HUNTING

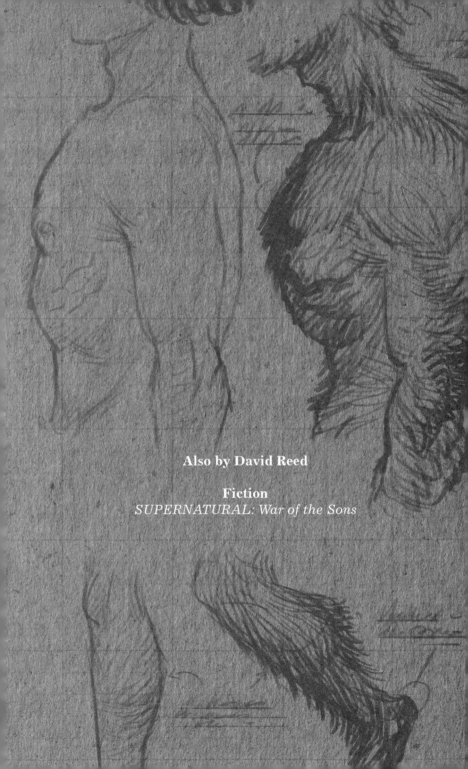

Also by David Reed

Fiction
SUPERNATURAL: War of the Sons

SUPERNATURAL™

BOBBY SINGER'S
GUIDE TO HUNTING

DAVID REED

SUPERNATURAL created by Eric Kripke
Art by Anthony Diecidue

it **books**

AN IMPRINT OF HARPERCOLLINS PUBLISHERS

*it*books

SUPERNATURAL ™ BOBBY SINGER'S GUIDE TO HUNTING. Copyright © and ™ 2011 by Warner Bros. Entertainment, Inc. All rights reserved. Printed in the United States of America. No part of this book may be used or reproduced in any manner whatsoever without written permission except in the case of brief quotations embodied in critical articles and reviews. For information address Harper-Collins Publishers, 195 Broadway, New York, NY 10007.

HarperCollins books may be purchased for educational, business, or sales promotional use. For information, please e-mail the Special Markets Department at SPsales@harpercollins.com.

FIRST EDITION

Designed by Timothy Shaner, nightanddaydesign.biz

Cover image courtesy of Warner Bros. Entertainment, Inc.

Library of Congress Cataloging-in-Publication Data is available upon request.

ISBN 978-0-06-210337-6 (pbk.)

16   OV/RRD   20 19 18 17 16

DEDICATED TO
MY MOM AND DAD,
FOR BUYING ME ALL OF
THOSE ACTION FIGURES.

CONTENTS

A Hole in My Brain. 1
The Banshee of Ashland 7
This Isn't Funny ! 23
Karen. 27
Demons 37
Angels 57
Anansesem 73
The Crusher. 93
And Then, I Ran 113
Nishigo Maru 119
Japan 155
Rufus 173
Something Good. 177
The Rules. 183
Where Am I Now?. 197
John Winchester 199
The Shit List 203
Tastes Like Chicken. 205
Alphas 213
Dragons 215
Names 219
Omaha 221
The Departed 225
Fried Foods. 231
Last Will and Testament 235
Sam and Dean. 237
Oblivion 247
The Hidden Memory. 250

ACKNOWLEDGMENTS

I'd like to thank Eric Kripke, of course, for creating *Supernatural* and hiring me to work on it, way back in season four, and Sera Gamble for not firing me when she took over the joint. I'd also like to thank Christopher Cerasi and Rebecca Dessertine—without them, I'd be publishing this on Internet message boards right next to pictures of Jared and Jensen with their shirts off. Maybe some of you would have preferred that. Lastly, I'd like to thank my wife, Mairin, and the rest of my family for putting up with me writing when I'm supposed to be watching the baby, cooking, cleaning, exercising, sleeping, and enjoying life.

HarperCollins would also like to thank Ant Diecidue and Mary-Ann Liu for the interior illustrations.

A HOLE IN MY BRAIN

I THOUGHT I'D DIE BLOODY.

Just seemed the likeliest way, given my line of work. I've looked Death in the face (literally . . . he's actually an alright guy), and, to be totally honest, I thought my ticket was gonna get punched a long time ago. I always figured there'd be some meaning to it . . . that my mark on this world would be more permanent than my blood stain on the floor. Instead, I'm gonna go out a gibbering turnip, mind so far gone that I won't be able to work a door knob, much less feed myself. Now there's a sobering thought—I'm gonna starve to death with half a cow in the freezer.

I should back up. This won't do any good if it doesn't make sense.

Three days ago—hell, maybe more, I can't be sure—I was in a place called Ashland, in northern Wisconsin. So far north, might as well be Canada. Town had a slew of disappearances and no leads. There was plenty of evidence, but the local PD just couldn't put two and two together.

Wait. I've gotta back up further.

My name's Bobby Singer. (At least I still remember that.) In all likelihood, you don't know me . . . because just about all my friends are dead and buried. As I said, it comes with the territory. If you're new to the game, I'll give you the basics: you know all that stuff that you were terrified of as a rug rat? The truly heinous stuff that'd send a chill from your ass to your elbows? Monsters, demons, the boogeyman under your bed—*it's all real*. I've seen it, I've hunted it, I've killed it. There're more people like me—hunters— but not as many as there used to be. Not near as many as there needs to be. Thanks to recent events, we're a dying species, and I'm the old breed. I've learned everything I can about every damned critter that walks, crawls, or flies, and I'm not gonna let that all be for nothing.

Back to Wisconsin. What seemed like an open-and-shut case . . . well, it must not have been. Last thing I remember, I had Ashland in my rearview mirror, heading west for Sioux Falls, where I planned on taking a long bath and watching as much trashy television as I could before the next catastrophe found me. Then, I woke up at home. Actually, "woke up" might be too gentle a phrase, as if I opened my eyes to the tweeting of birds as the sun rose—no, I scared myself awake, screaming bloody murder, damn near falling off the couch when I came to. Now, I won't lie to you . . . alcohol may have been a factor. Wouldn't be the first time that rotgut had done me wrong, but this felt different. The stabbing headache was present and accounted for, but something important was missing: *memories.*

It was random things, at first. Went to the kitchen, itching for a little hair of the dog, and the damnedest thing happened . . . I couldn't remember which one was the liquor cabinet. Again, you may not know me, but that's a big deal. Didn't take long to find it, but for that minute and a half the world was not right.

Taking stock of things, it was hard to ignore the grenade launcher lying on my living room floor. Not where I usually keep it. Must have been some bender. While trying to remember how it got there, I tidied up, carrying the guns and gear that were strewn all over the house to their proper places. The launcher belonged downstairs, in the basement armory lockup. As much as I wanted to keep it out as a conversation piece, house guests had a tendency to overreact to it. It's not like I used it for deer hunting, I have a semi-auto crossbow for that. Spinning the tumbler on the armory lock, my mind went blank. I'd opened that locker every day for over a decade, and suddenly couldn't recall the combination. Somebody's birthday, maybe? I tried my own, no dice. Tried a few other things, but let's skip to the punch line—twenty minutes later, I was down there with a blow torch and bolt cutters.

Something was wrong with me. I couldn't remember where I left my car keys; I couldn't even remember where I left my *car.* The driveway was empty. Whatever happened between Ashland and Sioux Falls had left a hole in my brain, and I was leaking memories. In my old life, when I was just Joe mechanic, the diagnosis woulda been Alzheimer's. But I ain't just Joe mechanic anymore, and everything I'd learned in twenty years on the job told me that this wasn't natural.

Only one thing to do: call the Winchester boys. Those two delinquents have a knack for getting out of messes when they've got no right to; seemed fair that they'd help me out of one for a change. Of course, to help me, they'd have to answer their friggin' phones. Those boys have more numbers than a Chinese phone book, but my calls went straight to voicemail on all of them. It'd be a hell of a lot easier to track them down if I could remember what direction they were heading last time I saw 'em, but life's not that easy. For all I knew they were upstairs, passed out themselves. After that occurred to me, I had to check every room of the house to make sure it wasn't true—I wasn't about to let those idiots sneak up on me if this was some kind of prank.

Turns out, it wasn't. There was no sign of the boys anywhere, no sign of my car anywhere, no clues as to where I'd been between Ashland and my house. In case you're not catching on to where this is going, I still have no friggin' clue. And it's getting worse. I tried to picture my mom's face this morning . . . couldn't.

Here's the rub—I don't know what happened to me. I don't know if I can fix it. But what I know for damn sure is that I'm not going down without a fight. I'm not letting everything I've learned disappear. So that's what you're holding in your hands— everything I know. Anything that'd be useful for the hunters that come after me . . . and that includes you, Sam and Dean. It's every hope I have of fixing the leak in my grapefruit. It's a guide to hunting. . . . It's a guide to *me*. My last will and testament.

THE BANSHEE OF ASHLAND

YOU KNOW THAT FEELING YOU GET when you're telling a story, and you know you're leaving the best parts out? That's my life now, 24/7. So I apologize in advance if I skip a juicy bit. I can't remember the things I can't remember, if you get my meaning.

Let me start by laying out my typical morning routine: wake up with the sun, give myself a once-over with the beard trimmer (next to godliness, and all that), get half-way done making breakfast . . . and then somebody calls with a catastrophe. You can set your watch to it—as soon as the eggs start scrambling, some fool needs my help. Often as not, it's Sam and Dean. They seem to get in more scrapes than most, which is saying something in this line of work. Up till a few months ago, Rufus Turner was the next most likely caller—rest his soul. The remainder of the calls are from other hunters across the country—across the world, now, if you count my buddy Eli in Budapest. Chased a vamp there, liked the food so much he never came home. Or was it the women?

Either way, his appetite is being satisfied. Most of the time, the caller just needs some lore. What do you use to kill a ghoul? What kind of critter sucks the salt right out of ya? That sort of thing. Other times, a hunter needs more . . . *direct* backup.

It came as absolutely no surprise, then, when I got a call last Thursday a.m., wondering if I'd come check out the disappearances of four men in Ashland. Who called me, that part is a blur. Must have been somebody I trust, though, or I wouldn't have made the drive. Believe me, there ain't much worth seeing north of Wausau. I got in the Chevelle, went east on I-90.

As I got close to Ashland, I started getting nervous. The Chequamegon forest just south of town is haunted, everybody knows that. What they don't know is that EMF is useless in the forest. For you baby hunters, EMF (electromagnetic field) meters are handheld doohickies that can sense when a ghost is present, or has been nearby recently. They're a hunter's best friend, saved my bacon more times than my butcher. As soon as you cross into the forest, the EMF meter lights up like Christmas, and not because of the spirits—because of the U.S. Navy. They got a transmitter at Clam Lake that talks to nuclear submarines, messes up our gear but good. That means you'll get no warning when the spirits get close, so watch your back. I wonder if that's why ghosts congregate there . . . because they like the friendly vibrations? Damn it, I'm getting sidetracked. *Ashland* . . .

The missing men were all upstanding types—paid their taxes, prayed regular, nice to their wives. Except for the youngest, that is, who hadn't yet settled down. I spoke to the wife of the first man to disappear, who might as well have been a brick wall. She had nothing but nice things to say about her dearly departed and no idea what'd befallen him.

The next gal, that's when I started getting someplace. She told me that her man had been hearing things before he went all Lindbergh Baby on her. But he wasn't hearing the usual stuff—voices, demonic instructions, none of it—he was hearing *singing*.

I talked to the young guy's mom, Bea Engstrom. The name stuck out, because the first girl I ever, well, *had relations* with, her name was Bea. That particular story doesn't need to go down in the historical record, though—her name may have been Bea, but she was a C+, max. Anyway, Bea told me the same thing, her son had been hearing singing. He couldn't get away from it, heard it in his apartment, at work, in the car, everywhere. It was a woman's voice, in a language he couldn't understand. Bea sent him to the doctor, thought something might be wrong with his ears. When he got a clean bill of health, he took to drinking, but that just made the singing worse. Five hours later, he was gone.

The last guy to disappear, a Mr. Lavery, his was the strangest case. He woke up one night at three in the morning, got in his car, and drove to the marsh fields outside of town. As he walked into the bog (still in his pajamas, mind you), a deer hunter spotted him, asked him what the hell he was doing. He couldn't answer. Just got back in his car and drove home. According to his wife, he had no clue what had compelled him to go out to the swamp, only that he knew he had to do it. Of course, when he up and vanished a day later, the first place they looked was the marsh. Police dogs came in all the way from Eau Claire, but never picked up his scent. Lavery never mentioned it, but I'd bet dollars to donuts that he was hearing the same singing voice, and that's what drove him to take a dip in the bog.

So, I ran down the clues:

SINGING THAT NO ONE ELSE CAN HEAR— this has been reported with ghosts on several occasions, most notably the case of Greta Wilson. Wilson was a famous opera singer in New York City in the thirties, known less for her vibrato than for her ample . . . assets. The lady was stacked, and had a rotating roster of gentlemen callers, one of whom didn't want to share, so he cut her throat when he found out that she'd been gettin' around. To an opera singer, that's the worst death imaginable—having your vocal chords slit. She couldn't even scream as she was being murdered. Lore says she haunted the back rooms of the club where she was killed, singing horribly (again, she was mostly known for her rack, not her warbling) in the ears of all the young ladies who were about to perform. Since Chequamegon is known to be haunted, singing ghost was my first guess in Ashland, too, except for rule *numero uno* with spirits: they don't travel. There are exceptions, but I'll get to that later. In this case, there was no evidence that the four missing men had been anywhere near each other in the days before their disappearances, so one ghost couldn't be at fault.

LURING PEOPLE TO THEIR DEATHS—this is a tactic used by crocotta, fierce little bastards who call people by name, often finding ways to convince the victim to kill themselves. Sam and Dean hunted one a few years back that was using telephone and Internet lines to pose as their victims' loved ones. Dean even got a call from John Winchester. Messed up stuff. The MO fit, but I'd never heard of a crocotta singing to their victims. Maybe this one was just big on musical theater, or maybe I was looking for something else entirely. Also, most victims of a crocotta are found dead, they don't just vanish.

THE SWAMP—that's the piece that made the puzzle fit together. Swamps are hotbeds of monster activity, for all the reasons you'd expect. They're wet, they're dark, humans tend to steer clear. This particular swamp was also *foggy*. I visited it my second day in town, when I ran out of other leads. The fog was heavy, the kind that makes you feel like you could suffocate in it. Like you're underwater on dry land. Now, I'm not what you'd call an international man—

I've been some places, but not near as many as I'd like—but that fog reminded me of a place I've seen a lot: the Guinness Brewery. Never been in person, but I've got a book in the bathroom about the world's most famous breweries. It's got a whole article about the history of Guinness, going back to 1759 when Arthur Guinness signed a nine thousand–year lease for his factory. That man had confidence in his product. One of the pictures in the book is of Arthur Guinness's country home on the east coast of Ireland, near a place called Swords (badass name, if you ask me). The house was swimming in fog; the same thick, impenetrable fog that covered the swamp in Ashland. Maybe that's where Guinness found inspiration for his beer.

FOG—the final clue. It rang one bell in my head, loudly: the Hag of the Mists, also known as a banshee. They're native to Ireland and Scotland, and manifest as an ethereal woman who *sings* to those about to die. The lore is sketchy at best, since they're awfully rare in the States, but most everything fit. Only, I can't remember a banshee actually killing anyone. They acted more as a warning—a harbinger that bad news was coming. I wondered if a banshee could be operating off the reservation, singing to a victim that she herself was about to kill? Wouldn't be the first monster acting squiggy this year. I never thought I'd see a *lamia* or an *okami* on this side of the pond, either.

One thing I didn't know about a banshee was how to kill it, so that meant research. This is an important lesson for the baby hunters out there, so listen (read . . . whatever) closely. It's all right in front of you. All the information you need, all the lore, it's staring you in your friggin' face, if you know what to look for. Try the local library, for example. "But they don't have a section on banishing Irish spirits," you whine. Yes they do, it's called the children's book aisle. Find a book of Irish folk songs, it'll give you just what you need:

> *Beneath the moon's bright eye /*
> *A woman softly sings /*
> *A warning to those who dwell /*
> *In the land of those not yet dead /*
> *Heed her voice /*
> *Or raise your iron.*
> > (Translated from Gaelic)

Plain as day. "Raise your iron," which I'm sure was prettier in Gaelic, means that they're vulnerable to iron, like most spirits. Of course, that didn't help me a lick. "Vulnerable to" isn't the same as "can be killed with." I could protect myself from the banshee, but had no idea how to permanently gank it. Back to the lore.

In a book of children's fables, I found a reference to the banshee. The kids in the story were frightened of hearing the banshee's song, since it meant that death would soon visit their family. One particularly terrified ankle-biter had heard the banshee's song before, when her grandmother died. She so feared hearing it again that she sang the banshee's song to herself every night, desperately trying to remember the words, so she'd recognize it if the banshee came once more. When the banshee did return, the little girl sang the song right back at the spirit—the banshee knew the song was being sung for her, and that her own time was at hand. She disappeared into the mists, and was never heard in those parts again. The *song* was the key. Repeat it back to the banshee and she'll be banished.

My first reaction: "Balls. I'm gonna have to sing."

Two challenges faced me: (1) getting the Banshee to target me, and (2) speaking Gaelic. I can read it well enough to translate the old documents, but saying it out loud? I was rusty, to say the least.

Ashland has a population of almost ten thousand—waiting around for the banshee to target me by chance wasn't going to work. I had to figure out what the connection between her victims was. All of them were men, so I had that going for me. They were between the ages of twenty-four and fifty-one. I was close enough to that. Three were white, one was Native American, so that didn't seem to be a factor. There's always a chance with these things that the vic pool is truly random. That's the worst possible situation for a hunter, since your only hope is to somehow catch the monster in the act, which in a town the size of Ashland or bigger is nearly impossible. A much better situation is when you can isolate what the monster is looking for in a victim, and make yourself the best possible example of that. Monster wants tall guys, you call Sam Winchester. Monster wants pretty girls, you . . . well, I don't know any of those. Guess I'd call Dean.

I took another look through the files of the missing guys, still got bupkis. Then I re-read my notes from talking to Bea, the youngest guy's mom. She'd left his room just as it was, in case he happened to just waltz back in like he'd never gone missing. Hanging from the wall was a deer hunter's orange vest. Not an uncommon sight in Wisconsin. Mrs. Lavery had told me that her husband was spotted in the marsh by a deer hunter. What if the victims were all deer hunters, and all of them had been hunting in the marsh in the days before their disappearances? The banshee might have spotted them, followed them home, then lured them back to her swamp.

I called Mrs. Lavery, found out the name of the hunter that'd stopped her husband from disappearing the first time: a man named Bill Henderson. Didn't take much effort to track him down at home, where he was holed up in his study, ashen and jumpy. "You been hearing things?" I asked him. The look in his eyes was enough to confirm my suspicions. The banshee was after him, already whispering in his ear.

You've got to jump on opportunities like that. A minute later, I had him surrounded by a pentagram of iron golf clubs, I'd salted the windows and doors (just in case), and I gave him an iron-pellet shotgun. If he heard the voice again, I told him to blast iron in the direction of the singing. With Henderson safe, I moved on to the next step: making myself a target.

I'd already been to the swamp, so I should have been familiar enough to the banshee. I walked out of Henderson's house, got several yards clear of any iron, and waited. If she couldn't get to Bill, I hoped she'd come after me instead.

Then I waited. And waited. And waited some more. The bitch musta really had her heart set on Bill Henderson. I decided to wait out the night in the backseat of my Chevelle, turned the radio on as I tried to fall asleep, but the song was weird. The words sounded like gibberish. Hell, it sounded like Gaelic—and that's exactly what it was. The banshee was starting in on me through the radio.

Overplaying your hand is easy to do as a hunter— you think you've got the critter figured out, you think you know all their strengths and all their weak- nesses, but often as not you've got big blind spots in the lore, and as soon as you come at the monster they'll throw a curveball. I wasn't going to run right to the swamp. I was going to play hard to get first. A leisurely breakfast at the local diner. A trip to the gun shop for some socializing. A stop at the liquor store to replenish my whiskey stores. All the while, I listened closely to the voice singing in my noggin, trying to make out and memorize all the words.

The banshee's warbling started to get to me—I felt a powerful compulsion to go down to the swamp, but held back as long as I could. Dinner at a French place—'cause I may not seem cultured, but it ain't all bratwurst and Budweiser at Casa Singer. And then, finally, I moseyed over to the swamp, to see about killing the banshee.

It was getting dark by the time I parked, which was regrettable but necessary. Spirits are most active at night, which should be obvious from every ghost story you've ever heard. Not that they won't rattle some windows during the day, but their main goal is scaring the piss out of everyone they can, and that's most effective at night. There's something primal about our fear of the dark—of the night. I've seen grown men whimper like babies when something makes a bump after the sun goes down.

I left my Chevelle in a gravel lot near the bogs. The lot was intended for hunters and wilderness-minded folks who wanted to spend a day in the Bad River watershed (where do they get these names?), but from the overgrown state of the place it was clear the lot wasn't used much. There was at least one other set of tire tracks in the gravel—maybe from one of the victims? But then where were their cars?. I brought a shotgun and enough iron shells to handle my business, then set out into the mire.

The beam from my flashlight started fritzing out, which is a surefire sign that otherworldly crap is about to go down—if there were cold spots (another solid indicator that there's spirit activity nearby) in the marsh, I wouldn't have known, the whole place was freezing as it was.

Then, I heard the weeping.

It wasn't like anything you've heard before, not like some teenager with a cheatin' boyfriend—this was a wail of anguish like what you'd hear in hell (wouldn't know about that myself, haven't been personally, but friends say it's not worth a visit).

Most of the bog was shallow water with long grass and trees growing out of the muck, but I came to a deeper section—more like a pond than a swamp. The wailing was coming from the middle of the pond, and I could have sworn that the water was bubbling at the center, like it was boiling. I trained my gun on the water, and turned to Sam and told him—

Wait.

Sam was there. Sam Winchester. What the hell is . . .

This isn't making any sense. Sam and Dean were there with me. They were hunting the banshee too. . . .

I turned to Sam, told him that the banshee was gonna come at us any second, to get ready with his phone, 'cause, see, I had sung the banshee's song onto the voice recorder on his iPhone doodad, and . . . this is all coming back in pieces, now. . . .

The banshee *did* come at us, but it wasn't what we were expecting. It was—there were two of them. A banshee and something else, something I've never seen or heard of before. A woman, but it was like she was liquid. Like a river flowing into the shape of a person.

How long were Sam and Dean with me? The whole time? I don't remember them being with me before the swamp. Did *they* call me to Ashland? Where the hell are they now? I'm calling them again. You can wait.

No answer.

Back to the banshee, and the . . . other thing. The banshee was singing, Sam hit play on his phone, my baritone rendition of the Hag's song came on, and . . . the thing smiled. Not the banshee, the other woman. The banshee splashed and flailed, sending water and steam flying in her death throes. Just like so many other critters that I ganked, she didn't go quietly.

Chunks of this are missing. Chunks of it don't piece together right. The other one, the river woman, she came at Dean, didn't even touch him and he ratcheted into a tree, pinned by nothing but the force of her mind. She hurt him bad, I could tell. Internal bleeding, maybe, but injuries like that are hard to suss out without a trip to the ER. Sam, being Sam, charged in like a bull and got himself thrown face-first into the water. It don't happen often, but I found myself frozen solid, took me a solid five seconds before I remembered I had a sawed-off in my hands. I pelted her with the chambered shell, didn't even make her flinch. That's when—she looked me in the eye. Like she recognized me. That look you get when you see something you've always wanted, and it's right there in front of you . . . like she wanted my head on a platter. And then . . .

I was here. On my couch.

I could've sworn I remembered the end of that story when I started telling it. I could have sworn Sam and Dean weren't in Ashland with me.

What is happening to me?

THIS ISN'T FUNNY

I JUST CALLED RUFUS'S CELL PHONE. Forgot for a minute that he was gone. Chances are, he wouldn't have been able to help me, but it'd do me some good to get all this off my chest—which I reckon is why I'm writing this.

I'm gonna get a drink

I'm back. Don't feel any better.

What do I do? Drive back to Ashland, find that bog? Use my fake FBI credentials to put out an APB on Sam and Dean, see if they turn up anywhere? I just . . . I can't shake the feeling that the answer's in my head, that I could fix this if I could just knock the right memory loose. Guess that means I've gotta keep writing.

Somewhere between the bog and here, I musta taken some kind of blow to the head. I musta lost my car. I musta lost Sam and Dean. If I can figure out any one of those things, maybe the rest will click into place. I got no clue on the *Total Recall* front, no answer from the Winchesters, so I guess it's time to LoJack my ride.

The Chevelle's been in my collection for decades, though it wasn't always my go-to vehicle. I got it as a junker, a total loss from some kid in Pipestone, Minnesota. He'd somehow managed to total the car while driving ten miles an hour in the parking lot of a grocery store. Takes ingenuity to be that stupid. The hull of the car sat in my junkyard (did I tell you I own a junkyard?) for near-on five years before I got the notion to rebuild it. If memory serves (and it hasn't, recently), I did it to impress a girl. Back in the day, it was a sight to see. Paint on the doors matched, no rust, no dents. As I got older, I got rougher around the edges, and so did the Chevelle.

That car has been with me for longer than any person I've ever known, if that gives you any clue as to how many years I've owned it. Longer than I knew my wife (may she rest in peace), longer than I knew Rufus or John Winchester. Longer than I knew my own mother. Right now, the Chevelle's not in the driveway—but I got back to Sioux Falls from Ashland somehow, and I ain't sprouted any angel wings, and I ain't got a bus ticket in my pocket. I think it's time to do a little junkyard reconnaissance, see if I can find any clues as to how I got here. If I don't finish this story, it's probably because I forgot why I was writing it.

. . . . .

It's worse than I thought.

Didn't notice it before, but at the front gate, some damn fool slammed into my Singer's Auto Salvage Yard sign, bent the supports back a ways, scraped some paint off—paint that matches the Chevelle's. Guess the idjit was me.

I followed the tire tracks into the junkyard, past a banged-up Chevy that I had up on blocks. Ain't on blocks anymore. Lucky it wasn't the Impala, or Dean would've had a fit. The tracks twisted around a bit, snaking to the back of the yard, where I found a crumpled up heap of metal. What used to be two cars is now one tangle of steel and glass—totally jacked. One of those cars used to be my Chevelle. How I walked away from that wreck, I can't even start to guess. I'd say I had a guardian angel on my shoulder—if I didn't know for a straight fact that angels are all rat bastards. Castiel being the exception who proves that particular rule.

That's all mysterious enough on its own, raises some questions I don't got answers to, but it's just the tip of the damn iceberg. What's really got me rattled is what I found next. Scratched out in big messy letters on what's left of the Chevelle's windshield—one word.

"Karen."

This ain't fair.

KAREN

I'M ALREADY PLAYING without a full deck, now they (or it, or whatever) are dragging my dead wife into things. My dead wife twice over, I should add.

Damn it.

"Karen" was written in giant letters on the windshield, and, as far as I can tell, I'm the one who drove the car back here. So what does it mean? Is it a warning?

Karen. What can I say about Karen? Do I write down the hunter version of my life with her, all the facts about the terrible thing that happened to her? Do I treat this like a "case"? Or do I use what might be my last words to write down everything she meant to me? Do I tell you that she spent so much time on her hair, getting it just right? That she'd find me on the couch after she took a shower, smelling like some kinda flower that I could never place—and that it's always the first thing I think of when I remember her? Or do I tell you that she taught me to cook, and that it changed my whole damn life? That she told me

27

to get over myself when I was mad about some stupid thing.

It all comes back to one question—do I think I'm gonna survive this? If not, then I may as well give you the sappy version. But I'm not near giving up. So I've gotta press on.

I met Karen when I was still a young man. I had ambitions like anybody else, but not huge ones. I wanted to work on cars. I wanted to be comfortable and done at five and have a beer in my hand by five-thirty. Not asking for that much, in the grand order of things. A simple life. First time I saw Karen, I regretted all of that. I wished I could have been somebody interesting from the city, somebody with a fancy job and a fat wallet. None of that mattered to her at all. "I thought you're giving us the non-sappy version, ya blowhard," you say. Yeah, this is going somewhere important, so quit yappin'. She wanted the simple life that I had. We were *happy* together, which is damn rare, if you ask me. Karen didn't want anything from me that I couldn't give her.

So when she came at me with a kitchen knife, I was surprised. Caught her hand just before she sank the blade into my chest; was so busy fighting her off that I didn't notice the stink of sulfur on her. All I could see was the little engraving on the knife's blade, near the hilt: "From Bobby." Now there's some irony or what have you—she was about to murder me with the knife set I gave her for Christmas. After I threw her clear I was able to get a good look at her.

She was the same woman I'd loved for years, but her eyes were black as a hole in the ground. Wearing the same clothes, the same earrings, but something deep inside had rotted out.

The thing that was possessing her didn't have a reason for comin' after me. It did it for the sick, lunatic fun of it. How it came to be in Sioux Falls, I'll never know. Pit stop on the way to the Pit, maybe. What was damn clear was that the thing wanted to play games with me before it killed me. A cat with a mouse. I'd like to think that I could have handled myself, even then, before I knew anything about the supernatural, but I won't lie to myself. I had no idea what I was facing, no clue what to do to protect myself. Kinda like my situation right now. The difference was, all I wanted to do was get Karen back. Because even if she killed me, I woulda spent eternity regretting not helping her. My wife was . . . broken, and I couldn't fix her.

I dodged the knife when she threw it, but that was just the beginning. She came at me with an axe, found one of my hunting rifles lying out—she wouldn't let up. *It* wouldn't let up, the thing inside her. No sugarcoating it, it was the worst day of my life, and I've seen downright godawful days.

So . . . I fought back. It took hours to accept it, but there it was. I told myself I had to do it, for her sake. I thought she musta been sick, something not right in her head. If I could just get her down, take her to the hospital, docs would figure out what was wrong.

But I had to get her down first, and I knew it wasn't gonna be easy. I had no idea.

I'd been hiding out in the junkyard. The evil son-ofabitch was inside Karen's mind, knew things she knew, but even Karen didn't know the ins and outs of the yard the way I did. When I decided it was time, I came back to the house, had a shotgun with birdshot loaded (pheasant season). I told myself I wouldn't have to use it, that the crazy would have boiled off by the time I found her. Wrong. When I found her in the living room, she had the butcher knife in her hand, the one with the engraving, and she was screaming like . . . like hell. It musta torn up her vocal chords something good to make that sound, but the bastard didn't care. I told her to drop the knife or I'd shoot. My hands were shaking so bad, it wouldn't take a four-year-old to tell you I was bluffing.

Then she turned the knife on herself. Pressed it against her skin, told me she'd gut herself if I came another step closer. Maybe you got a wife or a husband. Picture them giving you that choice. Tell me it don't eat you up, make the whole world seem . . . wrong.

I dropped my shotgun. Same as any man would do. Karen laughed at me. Cackled. The knife in her hand hanging low and deadly, ready to swing. I knew I had to get it from her, that I'd never have the upper hand as long as she had that knife. Shoulda taken a shot when I had the chance. Would have saved me from what happened next.

At the time, my house was different than it is now. Nowadays, it's mostly library, with the odd room having a sink or tub or bed mixed in with all the lore books, charts, maps, bibles, and holy books from every different church there ever was. Back then, it was a home. The living room was done up nice, with proper paint on the walls and furniture to match it. All of it Karen's doing. There was this one chair, called something French that I can't recall, that was her favorite. It stretched out just long enough for her to curl up and read a book on a lazy summer day. She'd get so caught up in the stories that the ice would melt in her tea before she took a sip. I had to throw that chair away on account of all the blood.

I moved as quick as I could, but she was faster, impossibly fast. My hands were on her arm, but my grip didn't hold the knife swung and tore into my left bicep. I've still got the scar where it sliced down. All I felt was a warm rush as blood soaked my whole left side, spurting in time with my heartbeat. Arterial. Deadly.

While I was distracted, she swung again. A jagged line carved into my chest, not deep enough to do any real damage, but scary enough to knock me on my ass. This woman was supposed to have my . . . this was Karen. And now my blood was on her face, and she was smiling a monster's smile, red specks on her pearl-white teeth. A shark, circling.

It took every ounce of strength I had to get back on my feet. And I don't mean physical strength, I mean I was ready to give up. I'da died, gladly, a hundred times over, to not have to do what I did to Karen.

She swung again, and I put my hand in front of the blade. My left hand, which was already close to useless 'cause of the blood loss. It wasn't so numb that I didn't feel the knife stick into my palm, though. The blade dug into my flesh, sent a shock down my spine, made my whole body light up with nerves I didn't even think I had, all of 'em screaming out with pain. But it worked. The blade stuck in my hand, and she was surprised enough that she hesitated before pulling it back out. I fought through the pain, pulled the blade outta my own hand—it was slippery with blood, my blood, and nearly spilled out of my good hand.

And . . .

I first saw Karen on a Sunday. She was wearing a sun dress, all flowery and young-looking, smiling with her cousin as they left service. The last time I saw Karen, she had a hole in her belly where I'd stabbed her. Not just once. Over and over, I . . . I lost control of myself. I don't get scared easy, but I was then—of course I was, she was the best thing that ever happened to me, and I was killing her. Even as I did it, I knew I'd never forgive myself.

But she didn't die, then. She rose up, blood pouring out of her like I'd opened a spigot in her chest, and came at me again. Using her fingers like claws on me as I stabbed her once more.

Another few seconds and she'd have killed me.

Lucky for me, she didn't have another few seconds. I'd heard a banging noise behind me while she was at my throat, but didn't pay any heed—I had bigger problems. When the window smashed open, it got my full attention. Through it, I saw a man holding a gun. In my state, I was sure he was there to arrest me for hurting my wife . . . then I looked up at her. Black eyes, covered in blood, grinning like a maniac—it wasn't my wife anymore. That was the moment I realized that the woman I married was already dead.

A second later the rock salt hit her. Flung her straight into the back wall, blood spraying all over the room, over her favorite chair. Steam hissed off her skin like she was a frying pan that was too hot to touch. The man shot her again for good measure. Had her cornered by the door to the kitchen, gore slicking the floor beneath her.

He pulled out a flask from his jacket pocket, doused her with it, and her skin charred like he had flung acid on her. For a second, that's what I thought he'd done. In the heat of the moment, I damn near threw myself in front of her . . . like I needed to protect the unnaturally possessed dead body of my wife. I couldn't see straight, much less think straight.

As Karen (the thing in Karen) sizzled in the corner, the man crawled in through the window. Grabbed her by the hair and dragged her like a rag doll into the kitchen, where he held her head under the sink. The whole while I was just standing like a mook in the living room, barely feeling my legs. I wouldn't feel so immobile again till the day I landed in a wheelchair, but that's another story.

Water sloshed out of the sink, almost boiling hot, as the man held Karen's head under the faucet. She resisted, but didn't seem to mind the waterboarding itself—until he started praying. I didn't understand a word he said at the time, but it was clearly some kind of religious rite. Like the old Latin masses I went to as a rug rat. I know now he was blessing the water, trying to drown her in holy H_2O. Whatever he was doing, it made her scream like . . . most people would say a banshee, but now I know better. Downright horrible, the noise she made.

Didn't take long before the thing inside her gave up, decided to make for more infernal pastures. She wrenched herself free of the man's grip, threw her head back and bellowed—belching out thick, oily black smoke. I understood immediately—the smoke *was* the thing possessing her, and it was leaving. It twisted through my kitchen with purpose, snaking past me and out the broken window, disappearing into the night.

Karen's body collapsed to the floor, dead as a stone. Cold to the touch, like she'd been dead for hours. I remember putting a hand on her belly, feeling the cold of her sticky blood on her dress. Didn't feel natural. Fingers touching the frayed hole where my knife had cut through fabric. I wanted to lie down next to her and die myself. I would've, too, if not for the man standing with a shotgun in my kitchen.

I didn't get even a minute to grieve before he was telling me what to do, telling me how we had to play the situation. How we could clean up the scene, make sure the blame didn't fall on me for her death. It was the last thing I was worried about. I just . . . I wanted to say goodbye to her. I wanted to know what the hell just came into my house and did this godawful thing to my wife. And here this bastard wants to talk about *disposing of the body*? I screamed at him. Said things that no sane man would say, because at the time I wasn't a sane man. And it wasn't a damn body, it was my *wife*. The last moment I'd ever have with her, and I spent it arguing with Rufus. Guess I didn't mention that yet. The day I met Rufus Turner was the day I had to kill my wife. Inauspicious start to a working relationship, if you ask me.

To this day, I can't remember exactly what I said to him. All I know is that words were exchanged, brief and angry, as I tried to explain what had happened, and he tried to explain what *really* happened. Rufus was already a hunter with plenty of notches on his shotgun, and knew a possession when he saw one. I was a mechanic who could only spit out gibberish. This'd be a good spot to tell you something about Rufus, but I think that'll have to wait. Till I've had more to drink, or I'm closer to being six feet under. Sore subject.

The one thing I *can* remember about our conversation is what he called the thing that possessed Karen: *demon*.

DEMONS

THERE'S A STORY I HEARD when I was little. About a boy who goes to his mother every night, tells her that a demon's outside his window. Every night, she tells him it ain't true, go back to sleep, try not to piss your sheets. The boy knows *something's* out there, so he gets a flashlight, goes out to find it. Stupid kid, you ask me. His mom catches him as he walks out the front door. Tells him to go back to sleep, don't let the bed bugs bite. Kid doesn't listen, ten minutes later is outside, looking for the demon. The happy ending? Kid was never heard from again. Moral of the story: listen to your mother. How's that for an uplifting children's yarn? Guess I had weird folks.

Demons are about as bad as bad gets. There's a good reason for it. Every demon was originally a *human* soul that was sent down to hell for whatever bad stuff they did while they were living. Hell is not a fun place, and I have a few friends who can attest to that. It twists you, breaks you, squeezes you, like coal into a diamond, except the ugliest, meanest, cruelest diamond you've ever seen. Was that not a clear analogy? Whatever. No human deserves to become that, no matter what messed up crap they did on earth.

The native form of a demon is black smoke, like that monster on *LOST*. Maybe they were clued in to real demon lore when they made that up. Happens more than you'd think. In case it wasn't clear from my Karen story, demons possess a human by entering their mouths. Like barfing, but in reverse. Sick stuff. You taste the sulfur for days. Right, that reminds me—

Demonic signs:

- **Sulfur.** If you're investigating a suspicious death or disappearance, first thing to look for is sulfur. Demons leave it behind when they smoke in and out of bodies, through windows—anytime they come in contact with physical objects. Luckily, sulfur smells like balls—easy enough to find in a crime scene.

- **Lightning storms.** It's hard to tell whether a lightning storm is a demonic omen or just bad weather. Both happen often enough that it's usually worth checking up on areas that have had dry lightning, looking through the newspaper and seeing if anything else suspicious is going on. Like:

- **Cattle mutilations.** Not sure what they're doing with those cows, but all the cattle mutilation stories in the *Bumfuck Nebraska Post* aren't 'cause of little green men, it's 'cause of demons. Far as I've heard, they don't get anything advantageous out of it. Wouldn't be surprised if they do it to pass time, or just to confound us.

Lore on demons goes waaaay back. Cave paintings of stick figures show black smoke pluming out of people's mouths ... friggin' Barney Rubble was drawing demons on the walls of his house thousands of years before humans discovered agriculture. If that doesn't tell you how ingrained in our culture these things are, nothing will. Demons are the anti-human— they're what happens when we're not governed by a conscience, the rule of law, community ... they're the worst parts of us, amped up a thousand times.

Biggest identifying mark? Black eyes. Not just the iris, the whole shebang. They're capable of hiding their black eyes and revealing them when they choose, but there are certain times when they can't help but show their true color (or lack thereof). When an angel is in their presence, when they hear the name of God (they *really* don't like Jehovah), when

they're splashed with holy water . . . plenty of ways. Problem is, identifying the demon is usually the least of your worries.

Most demons are confined in the Pit. There are ways in and out, but it's tricky; the average demon can't swing it on their own. Most demons wandering topside got their ticket punched by a hellspawn way high up the pay scale, somebody the likes of Azazel (also known as the Yellow-eyed Demon), Alastair or Lilith. Once they're out of hell, they scud around in their smoke form, looking for a human meatsuit to possess. I've even heard of a demon possessing an animal, but that's a rare case. (Also heard about an animal's spirit possessing a human, but that's a looong story, and best told by Sam and Dean, who lived it.) Demons don't need permission to possess someone, but there are certain tricks to avoiding it. First off, strong-willed folks are less susceptible to it in general. It's your weakness that demons thrive on, since that's what they're made of in the first place. A demon is nuthin' but a human soul that was too weak to keep resisting the torment of hell. Makes sense that they'd have trouble possessing someone with stronger will. 'Course, there's demons out there that'll bore their way into your skull no matter how tough you are. The good news is that there are symbols and sigils you can use to prevent possession. Here's a symbol the boys have tattooed on their chests, keeps all but the most powerful demons out.

Now, the most important thing to know about demons? They might as well be the Terminator. You can't just shoot one in the head and expect it to go down. They're tough in a way that almost no other creatures are, because the demon's soul isn't bound to the meatsuit in the same way a human's is. If a human's body dies, their soul leaves. If the body a demon's in gets damaged, the demon will hold it together through force of will alone. Shot, stabbed, dropped out a window, you name it, they'll live through it—but there's a big catch. All of those injuries are still affecting the poor sap whose body the demon is riding around in. The minute the demon leaves, the body falls apart. That's what happened to Karen. Had I only known, my life'd be a lot different. I'd be. . . . Well. Let's leave it at different.

Depending on the pay grade, demons can manifest different abilities, but here's the basic set:

- **Superhuman strength.** No matter the size or strength of the human they're possessing, a demon brings with it an impressive set of guns. I've been on the receiving end of enough demon beat-downs to know that their strength comes from something supernatural, some magical connection to forces we can't see or understand. Yoda meets the Incredible Hulk.

- **Telekinesis.** This one's not factory standard, it's more an aftermarket upgrade thing. Some demons, if they're powerful enough, can move things with their minds. And by "things," I really mean me, Sam, and Dean, and by "move," I mean "smash."

All that being said, they also have vulnerabilities up the ying yang:

- **Devil's trap.** A symbol similar to the warding tattoo, the "devil's trap" is about as old a hunter trick as there is. Once a demon enters a devil's trap, they can't step outside of it—or leave the body they're possessing. Very helpful when you need to get some answers from one of the slippery bastards. They're only freed once a line of the trap is broken. Memorize the symbol. Right now.

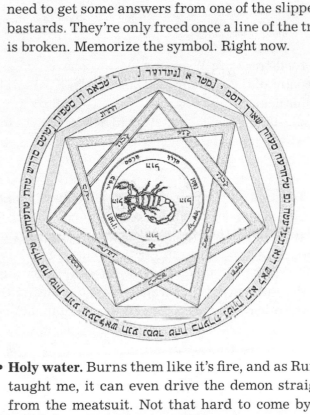

- **Holy water.** Burns them like it's fire, and as Rufus taught me, it can even drive the demon straight from the meatsuit. Not that hard to come by in most towns, either. Contact the local priest, see if they're willing to bless a couple gallon jugs, keep 'em in your trunk. It'll save your ass one day, I guarantee it. If the padre won't play ball, I'll leave it to you to decide whether stealing sacred water from a church is karmically kosher, provided it's gonna be used for smiting hell folk.

- **Iron.** Demons can't cross an iron line, and it burns them almost as bad as holy water. Samuel Colt famously built a devil's trap out of iron railroad tracks in Wyoming, with a church on each point of the pentagram. Damn near impenetrable for demons, and for good reason—at the center of the devil's trap is a gateway to hell itself. The only way to open the gate is with the Colt, which, now that you mention it:

- **The Colt.** It's a gun that can kill anything. One bullet, one dead critter. Except, of course, for the exceptions that prove the rule. Sam and Dean tried busting a cap in Lucifer, barely gave him a headache. He said that he was one of "five things the gun can't kill," which probably means that the other three archangels (Gabriel, Raphael, Michael) and God round out the list. Or maybe he was lying. He's Satan, after all. Can't be trusted to tell you the time. Either way, any run-of-the-mill demon will spark out like a flashbulb if they're hit with a bullet from the Colt. 'Course, that means their human host will die as well, but there are times when it's the only option. Samuel Colt built the gun in 1835, basing it on his Colt Revolver design. I've got no idea what kind of extra mumbo jumbo he had to throw in to give the gun its everything-killing mojo. Text on the side is Latin, *non timebo mala*. "I will fear no evil." Sorry to say, the Colt is one of a kind. It was last seen in Carthage, Missouri, but I wouldn't bother looking for it . . . its last owner was none other than the Devil himself.

- **Exorcism.** This is a biggie. Demons are tied to their hosts tenuously, and with the right Latin you can break that connection. Force them back to the Pit. Hopefully, you're able to trap the demon and say the incantation before the host's body is damaged. The full text is long—so long that you're likely to die of boredom before you finish off the demon. Luckily, there are a few juicy phrases that seem to do the trick without all the fat—credit goes to Dean Winchester for this abridged version.

    Exorcizamus te, omnis immundus spiritus.
    Omnis Satanica potestas, omnis incursio
    infernalis adversii. Omnis congregatio
    et secta diabolica, ergo, draco maledicte
    ecclesiam tuam. Secura tibi facias libertate
    servire, te rogamus, audi nos.

    If that don't work, *run*.

- **Salt.** Kinda like iron, salt drives demons crazy. They can't cross a line of the stuff, which is more important than you'd think. Of all this crap, salt is the most likely to be stocked in the average house / office / demon-infested riverboat casino (hey, it happened once). Draw a line around yourself or whatever bystanders you're trying to protect, the demon can't get to 'em. Of course, that won't stop a demon from dropping a piano on someone inside a salt line, or, you know, just *shooting* them, but it's a start. Another tool of the trade—rock salt shotgun shells. They're just regular shells with the buckshot traded out for salt. Does the trick.

- *Palo santo.* Holy wood. Don't snicker, this is serious. *Bursura graveolens* is the Latin name. It's a special type of wood that, if you sharpen it up right, can be used as a stake to pin down a demon. It won't kill 'em, but it'll sure rile 'em up good. It's not common in the States, so you'll have to go out of your way to find any. But if you find yourself in South America, keep an eye out for it. Also, watch out for a broad named Lucinda Los Diablos, a lady who runs a, uh . . . massage house in Lima. *Pretty* sure that ain't her real name, but it sure as hell describes her personality.

- **Ruby's knife.** Now this is a long damn story, and I don't think it'll do any of us good for me to repeat the whole thing, so here's the CliffsNotes version—Sam Winchester is an idiot. Okay, I take it back. He may be the smartest guy I know, it's just . . . his taste in women leaves something to be desired. He's got too much heart for his own good. There was this demon named Ruby that Sam took to when she promised to help him keep Dean from getting sent to hell. "But she was a *demon*," you're saying. Yeah, I was saying the same thing. Sam trusted her, and for one big reason—she was just as likely to gank a demon as Sam and Dean were. Turns out there's infighting even in hell, and for a long time it seemed like Ruby was on our team. She carried a special knife that had the same effect as the Colt on demons. A fatal strike with the knife would kill the demon—not sending them back to hell—*killing* them. Do not pass Go, do not collect two hundred quatloos. Dean saw through the demon bullcrap and used the knife on its owner, killing Ruby with it when she turned out to be (of course) playing Sam. Nowadays, Sam usually carries the knife, but he and Dean switch off as need be. I recently sussed out that Samuel Colt may have been responsible for the knife's construction—wonder how many other monster-killing weapons are out there made by his hand. If I die, somebody better go through my junk and find Colt's journal, then read it cover to cover.

- **The word of God.** Demons don't like God, not one little bit. I know, very surprising. Any of His names will cause a demon to flinch and involuntarily flash their black eyes. It's painful to them, but nothing like iron, salt, or any of these other things. Won't send them running, but it'll get them off your back for a bit.

- **Hex bags.** Usually the tool of a witch or warlock, hex bags can also be used to shield a person from demon radar. Demons will use location spells to track down people they're after, and often enough they're after hunters, so this is an important one. Here's the recipe:

    Two bones from a chicken's foot.
    An unbroken spider's egg.
    Lavender and hemp (Cannabis sativa—*and no funny business, people*) *in equal amounts. Don't matter how much, just as long as they're equal.*
    Something to do with goofer dust. *Right? No. Goofer dust keeps hellhounds at bay, and is also used in . . . I can't remember. Damn. Guess you'll have to find somebody with a working thinker to tell you the rest of the recipe.*

Hex bags can also be used for more offensive purposes, but I won't get into that. That kinda magic is dark and will eat away your soul if you dive too deep into it. If there's one thing I've learned about magic in general, it's that there's a cost to it—a consequence to every magical action you take. You want to stay on the good side of that line, or you'll end up just like the things you're trying to hunt. Speaking of, that brings us to the final demon vulnerability:

- **Sam Winchester.** The most powerful weapon I've ever seen used against a demon? The mind of Sam Winchester. Let this be a cautionary tale. Sam has abilities like you wouldn't believe, but they're like a car engine—they require a lot of fuel. The fuel that drove his engine? Demon blood. Drinking it gave him sway over demons, let him fling them around in the same way they usually fling *us* around, but he could do way more than that—he could drain the life out of them just by lookin' at 'em. But like I said, there was a price. You can't drink that kind of demon blood without becoming a little bit demon yourself. Sam's clean now, but he went through hell to get that way—twice. Trust me, you do not want to go through demon detox. And don't think you can just go drink a little demon blood yourself and get those same powers, don't work that way. At least I don't think it does. Never been dumb enough to try myself.

All this applies to your everyday demon, but that's not all there is. There're types that are way, way worse. Taxonomically speaking, the easiest way to tell the difference is by eye color. Black eyes are the garden-variety. Then there's:

- **Red eyes.** Most folk call these crossroads demons,

'cause of their MO. They're summoned by humans at a crossroads to act, basically, as genies. You make a wish, they grant it, but the price is steep. Most demon deals are for ten years, and at the end of that period they come back to collect what they're owed: your soul. Now, I can't say that only idiots would ever make a deal like that, because I'm guilty of it myself. There were extenuating circumstances, ya see. And I got the pink slip back for my soul, so no harm no foul, but it's a slippery damn slope. In this line of work, you get into situations with no clear exit, and you'll be tempted— especially since crossroads demons have power beyond what you'd think is possible. All the stuff that Aladdin's genie couldn't do, like bringing people back from the dead, making them fall in love with you, the whole deal, they can do it.

A smug Irish bastard named Crowley is the king of the crossroads demons, and he'll lord that over you every time you meet him.

- **Orange eyes.** Haven't encountered one myself, but I've heard stories about an orange-eyed demon who raised hell back in the seventies. Her thing was to take over the bodies of newly married women and use 'em to murder their husbands. Couple of the guys lived, said their blushing brides flashed orange eyes then went *Psycho* on them. Similar enough to Karen's case, but I know for a fact that demon had black eyes. Even in my current predicament, with the memories dripping right outta my skull, I could never forget that sight.

- **Blue eyes.** A demon named Samhain had blue eyes, was the only one of that type I've ever heard of. The raising of Samhain broke one of the sixty-six seals—the seals that were keeping Lucifer chained up in his coop, so it should be plenty obvious that Samhain wasn't a great guy to be around. If you're an omen of Satan's imminent arrival, you're bad news, period. Sam and Dean took Samhain down, but not before witnessing his abilities— summoning revenants (zombies, more or less) and unleashing a blast of white energy. Luckily, Sam was hopped up on demon blood at the time, so he was able to resist the effects of that energy. It was awfully similar to the abilities of . . .

- **White eyes.** Lilith and Alastair being the prime examples. Alastair was hell's chief interrogator, and by that I mean torturer. When Dean Winchester was in the Pit, it was Alastair who put him on the rack every day. Lilith was, well, the demon bride of Satan, if that puts an image into your mind. She was the one pulling the strings on Lucifer's jailbreak. Also, she ate babies. Not kidding. Both of those yahoos are dead now, so at least there's that. They were far more powerful than any black-eyed demon I've ever seen, and had some special skills, like that white energy blast that Samhain could pull. Both Lilith and Alastair were impervious to devil's traps, Ruby's knife, salt, iron, the works. They both were resistant to Sam's psychic power, at least until he really went overboard and drank a couple gallons of demon blood. Then he popped 'em like lightbulbs on concrete. If you encounter a white-eyed demon, your best bet is to call a Winchester or run like hell. *Do not* engage one by yourself. *Do not* try to exorcise them, that'll just piss 'em off. Lilith was the very first demon ever created (by Lucifer himself), and as such was incredibly powerful. Lore says there are at least two more white-eyed demons out there, though they may well be shuttered up in hell at the moment. I hope for humanity that they are.

- **Yellow eyes.** Saved the worst for last. A yellow-eyed demon named Azazel set in motion a lot of things for me, Sam, and Dean; for the whole world, really. He was part of the plot to raise Lucifer from his cage—his job was to make sure that Sam was in place to break the final seal (killing Lilith). He made demon deals with desperate women—gave them whatever they needed in exchange for the right, ten years later, to come to their homes and feed his own blood to their infant children. Sam Winchester was one of those kids. Azazel did more than just feed Sam demon blood, though—he killed

Mary Winchester and started John on his path towards becoming a hunter. The other children Azazel visited also developed special abilities, and eventually were pitted against each other in a fight to the death. Long story short, Dean avenged his mom's death, put a Colt bullet right in Azazel's grapefruit. Luckily for us, Azazel's the only yellow-eyed demon ever referenced in the lore books.

One last wrinkle in the demon lore—the Croatoan virus. You've heard of Roanoke, right, one of the first European colonies in the Americas? Everybody in the village goes missing mysteriously, leaving just the word "Croatoan" carved on a tree? A demonic virus was responsible for their disappearance—or "demonic germ warfare," as Sam likes to call it. Basically, it's the monster plague. Turns people into demonic zombies, hungry for violence. It spreads through blood-to-blood contact, which, when they're as bite-happy as Croatoan demons are, is pretty much inevitable. The good news is that they're way easier to kill than a regular demon, though that's not much consolation for the person that was infected. A shot to the head should take care of it, but I'd double-tap, just in case. Part of Lucifer's plan to rid the earth of humanity was to unleash the Croatoan virus through a swine-flu vaccine—luckily, we caught wind of the plan and were able to stop it before the real damage was done, but man, it coulda been bad. End of days bad. Because here's the rub—there may be millions of demons out there, somewhere . . . but most of them are locked up tight in hell, and those walls are pretty secure. Only a small percentage get to walk the earth. But with Croatoan, the potential's there for a demon *army*, numbering in the hundreds of millions. Instead of letting a soul bake in hell for a few hundred years before it turns into a demon, you just gotta expose them to the virus, and blammo. Demon. And there's no cure for it, no way back. The scariest part . . . I got no clue what happens to the human soul inside when it's exposed to Croatoan. There's a chance, and it's just my own theory, that Croatoan is the equivalent of poison for the soul. Rots you out from the inside. You could be the most pious, God-fearing guy on the block, and one drop of infected blood condemns you to an eternity in hell. Tell me that ain't scarier than . . . just about anything.

I need another drink.

I'm sure I'm forgetting something . . . hopefully not the part that'll save your ass if you run into one of these yourself. Should get back to the problem at hand. Memory. Demons have the motive, for sure—they'd jump at any chance to mess with a hunter—but do they have the means? Alastair, Lilith, Azazel, Crowley, they've all shown that they have the power to do things far greater than a regular demon, but could they really put a tap into my brain and suck out the juice? I've been going through my sources as I put this together, and nothing points to them having that kinda power.

But that don't answer the big question—why the hell is "Karen" scratched into the Chevelle's windshield? What connection could there be? Could it be *that* demon, the one that Rufus ripped out of Karen, come back for round two? There's just no way to know, not without more evidence.

You get now that demons are threat-number-one to humanity, but, I've got a nagging tickle in the back of my head, tellin' me I might be looking in the wrong direction on this one. That I shouldn't be looking down . . . I should be looking *up*.

ANGELS

UNTIL SEPTEMBER 2008, I woulda told you that angels were a myth. Demons were real, monsters were real, ghosts were real, hell was real, but the only thing standing up for the side of good was mankind. Kind of a depressing worldview, but that's what the evidence showed. Though in a way, it was almost comforting—there was nothing out there gonna save us but us, and that made us important. It gave us purpose, activated our survival instincts—it's the reason there are hunters. If there were angels up there making sure things were fair and balanced, we could all sit poolside drinking booze with little umbrellas in it and enjoying the scenery.

There are angels, but I'm not in Cabo working on my tan, so how do you square those two facts?

Angels are dicks.

←——Yeah, even He-Man there.

In the grand scheme of things, everybody looks out for themselves, and you'll never learn anything truer than that. Everybody's actions are steeped in their own interests, even angels'. They may have been created to serve God *and* man, but since God flew the coop . . . they've been following the letter of divine law, not the intent. They were created before us, but weren't given free will. Bummer for them. Ever since, a certain heavenly contingent has been on the warpath, determined to wipe us off the planet so that they can come in and enjoy the paradise that God created for us. A couple of us talkin' apes stood up for ourselves (with the help of an angel named Castiel who turned against his brothers) and we've (at least for now) stopped the great planetary enema of 2010 from moving forward. So, humans are *still* pretty much the only force in the universe standing up for humans, but that's probably how it should be.

Why do I bring the winged bastards up? Because they're the most powerful things out there, and the only ones that I know for a fact can mess with a man's memory. An angel named Zachariah made Sam and Dean think that they were peons in a big architecture firm for a week. Castiel wiped away all of Lisa and Ben Braeden's memories of Dean—that was at Dean's request, once he realized that knowing him was just gonna get them hurt, or worse. So I know they have the hardware to blot out memories, though I can't for the life of me figure out why they'd be targeting me. The Apocalypse was called off. That war's over.

Unless—maybe I learned something that I wasn't supposed to. Maybe, between Ashland and here, I saw something, read something, figured something out that turned the tables on the whole thing, and now they're cleaning up the mess? No—because if angels are one thing, it's *orderly*. My mind right now, it's the opposite. When they messed with Sam and Dean's memory, they did a bang-up job, made them really believe that they weren't brothers, that they'd had entirely different lives than the ones they actually have. If an angel was behind this . . . I have to think they'd have done a better job, left my brain in better condition. Left fewer holes.

But it's an interesting thought, isn't it? That I saw what I wasn't supposed to, and somebody's making sure that I don't remember it?

For the record, I've tried to contact the one angel I'm on speaking terms with, Castiel, and heard nothing back. He's busy fighting a war in heaven, so . . . Guess my problem is small fries compared to that.

It's been close to forty hours since I slept. I should shut my eyes for a bit, see if that doesn't clear some of this up. I'll come back to this once I can see straight.

. . . . .

Nope. Sleep's not happening. It's about three in the morning now, and I'm wired. I went back out to the junkyard, looked through the car again for clues. Found a few receipts in the glove compartment (a guy's gotta write off his business expenses), all of them from Ashland, all from before I went back to the swamp. Either I didn't stop for food on the way back to South Dakota, or I was messed up enough to not care about lowering my tax liability—and I'd have to be pretty messed up for that. Also, some of the receipts were for three meals, which means . . . Sam and Dean were there, maybe the whole time. Why is it I can picture parts of it so clearly but can't remember who was with me? I mean, I was there to . . . wait. Why did I go to Ashland?

I just re-read what I wrote about the banshee, almost none of it rings a bell, now. More stuff's leaking out. Balls.

I have to blast through this, quick and dirty. Get what I know out there before I don't know it anymore.

Angels.

They're not the "fluffy wings and harps" types you see on Christmas cards. Angels are divine warriors, soldiers of God—His own heavenly army. Think the Mossad, but with a worse sense of humor. Or God's Secret Service, including the suits. Their power can't be overstated. They do have wings, but they're not visible to humans—while on earth, they use human vessels to move around, like demons. Most of the time, they look like trench coat–wearing mooks.

Their abilities:

- **Unimaginable physical strength.** They can take a licking and keep on ticking. Only the highest level demon stands a chance in a physical fight with an angel. No human dare even try. Bullets, devil's traps, iron, salt . . . none of it will even ruffle their trench coats. I tried every mystical warding symbol I knew, none of them stopped Cass from walking in the door when Dean and I first met him.

- **Smiting.** Angels can kill with a touch of their fingers—and some of them don't even need the touching part. Works on humans, demons, monsters, whatever. If it's alive in any sense of the word, you bet your ass an angel can kill it. Zachariah gave Sam stomach cancer with a snap of his fingers. Took away his lungs with another snap. You don't fight angels. You find a way to have leverage over them, or you get killed by them. Even their appearance is deadly. When Pamela Barnes used a séance to spy on Castiel's true form, it burned the eyes right out of her head. When Cass spoke to Dean with his true voice, he shattered glass and nearly popped Dean's eardrums.

- **Teleportation.** As I said, they're not fluttering around on little angel wings. When angels want to go someplace, they just *go*, appearing instantly out of the ether. That can be both helpful and damn annoying, since they can appear when they're called immediately, but they also can leave without so much as a tip of the hat. And just try fighting something that can appear behind you right as you're swinging your blade.

- **Telekinesis.** Same as with the high-level demons, angels can manipulate the stuff around them with their minds. Fling people into walls, send out blasts of psychic energy, pick up cars and break 'em in half . . . it'd be impressive if they were on our side. Since most of them aren't, it's just scary.

- **Time travel.** One of the many ways angels dick around with human civilization: messing with our history. Angels have the power to go back in time and change things, though they claim that history is already written and that we all have a destiny and blah blah blah whatever. Same angel that told Dean Winchester he couldn't go back to save his mother from being killed sent another angel back in time to un-sink the *Titanic*. Time is flexible. Certain things will always be the same (the sky will always be blue, steak will always be delicious) but some things are up for grabs. Little things, like who's alive and who never existed. Who lives happily ever after and who ends up alone with a bottle of whiskey at a piece of crap Wang PC, typing out the sum total of his life's experiences in the hope that somebody will read it and . . . never mind. Angels can time travel. That's all you really need to know.

- **Omniscience.** Don't know how they do it, but angels have a way of keeping tabs on a lot of things at once. Like, say, every activity in an entire town, down to the smallest detail. There are limits, of course, and they can't be everywhere at once, but it's downright creepy how *aware* they are sometimes. Don't think you can cross an angel and get away with it.

- **Dream visitation.** Say you've found a way to hide yourself from an angel (I'll get to that in a bit)— but the angel still wants to have words with you. Likely they'll just pop into your dreams and scare the pants off you just as you're getting cozy with Tori Spelling.

- **Healing powers.** I have to say, this one I like. Angels have the power to raise the dead and heal any injury, though it requires a lot of celestial energy. That's how Castiel brought Dean back from hell . . . and how Cass brought me back from the dead after Lucifer snapped my neck. Don't expect them to be that benevolent for you. Most angels would sooner blast your corpse out of existence rather than help you out.

- **Liquor tolerance.** Cass can hold his liquor. 'Nuff said.

- **Memory alteration.** Like I said. Far as lore I've seen goes, angels are the only critters that can muck around with a man's memory. 'Course, I've got hundreds of lore books I've never even opened, especially since I inherited the Campbell family hunting library a few months back. One thing did strike me, however—if an angel was really this gung-ho about line-item vetoing my memories, you'd think they woulda blacked out my memories of angels screwing with people's memories, too. You know, so I wouldn't even suspect 'em. Huh.

One important thing to remember about angels— their power isn't baked in, it's . . . how do I explain this? An angel in a vacuum is no more powerful than a human. Their, uh, *potency* . . . comes when they're backed up by the full power of heaven. See, angels act as . . . sorta like *channels* for heavenly power. An angel is like a fire hose. If the spigot's turned off and no water's flowing, they can't get anything done. But once the valve's opened and water's flowing . . . ya understand? And heaven, in this analogy, is the great big water tower in the sky, full of energy. That power comes from souls—human souls, which they harness like little nuclear reactors to light up heaven and wage their eternal war with hell. Wait. I thought the metaphor was about water, not electricity. Whatever. The more souls are in heaven, the more powerful they are. That's what makes their apocalyptic plans so damn shortsighted—how are they supposed to replenish their power source if they kill off all of us low dwellers? Idjits.

On that topic . . . for two thousand years they left us to our own devices. Then the rumblings of the Apocalypse started and they came back to earth to help push things along. They *wanted* the Apocalypse, so they could have a final battle with Lucifer and take earth for themselves. One of 'em in particular was pushing for the prize fight—Michael.

Michael's an archangel, the top tier, the most powerful. There were four archangels—Michael, Lucifer, Raphael, and Gabriel. Now, Michael and Lucifer are locked up together in a cage in hell, Gabriel's dead, and Raphael . . . he's (I guess it's she, now—switched vessels) *she's* locked in a civil war for control of heaven. Heavy stuff.

Archangels are way more powerful than rank-and-file angels, and are assigned special duties, like protecting prophets of the Lord from harm. Far as I can tell, the powers of an archangel are on par with that of God near limitless. That's not to say that they're invincible. Gabriel was killed by Lucifer, so that don't really count, but they *are* mortal beings. Just, you know, mortals that have been alive for eons and who channel the energy of God Himself.

There are also other tiers of angels, like the cherubs—that's what Cupid is. They're assigned to fulfill divine will by arranging love connections on earth. Keep that in mind the next time you see a looker across the bar—you might be getting played by a cherub. John and Mary Winchester were, according to Cupid, an arranged couple. All part of the heavenly plan, fulfilling their destiny, yada yada yada. Two sides of the same coin—the hunter family and the Michael Sword, combining to form two brothers who could fulfill their bullcrap prophecy. Light and dark, yin and yang, Dean and Sam. If I've learned one thing from my dealings with angels, it's that there's no such thing as destiny. Just choices that you can have thrust on you, or make for yourself.

Know this—if you do choose to defy an angel, get ready for the fight of your life. Keep these things in mind, they might just save you from getting your head shoved up your ass:

- **Permission.** This is their Achilles' heel. Unlike demons, angels need permission to take control of a host. It seems like a small thing, but it makes all the difference in the world. They can't jump from meatsuit to meatsuit willy-nilly, and their list of potential vessels isn't limitless. There's a bloodline of angel vessels, descended from who knows where, and if those vessels say no, the angels are stuck floating around like a fart in the wind. Certain angels require more powerful vessels, like the archangels. Not just any human is built tough enough to contain Lucifer or Michael, and that's where Sam and Dean fit into the plan. They were supposed to be the hosts for Lucifer (Sam) and Michael (Dean) for their final battle, the one that'd take out half the earth. But they didn't count on Dean and Sam showing some backbone and saying *no*. That may be their fatal flaw—angels rely on humans to go along with their plans, but humans have that which angels lack . . . free will.

- **Angelic blades.** A weapon that all angels carry, an angelic blade is shorter than a sword, but longer than a dagger. They're effective against almost anything, including angels themselves. It'll take a direct blow to be fatal, but it can be done. Dean killed Zachariah with one. The problem is that they're not easy to come by. Black market occult arms dealers are out there, but none of them stock angel blades. Unless you happen upon a dead angel, you're not likely to ever encounter one of their blades, except if you find yourself at the pointy end of one.

- **Enochian.** Normal black magic doesn't affect angels, so you have to dig a little deeper. Turns out you just have to be speaking the right language. Enochian is the native spoken and written language of angels, and has its own symbology and phonetics that can be used in a whole mess of spells, like:

- **Banishment sigil.** Learned this one from Castiel. It's a little tricky, since it has to be written in *blood*, but that's magic for you. Once you've scratched out the basic form of the symbol, you place your bloody hand right in the center to complete the banishment ritual. Any angel (this works on all of them, from cherubs to archangels) in the area will be blasted to the next time zone. (Or dimensional realm, I don't know. They're not in the room any more, and that's good enough for me.) Interesting to note—this works with both human and angelic blood. Probably works with demon blood, too. Might be worth experimenting, seeing which kind is most effective.

- **Warding inscription.** Couldn't replicate this one myself, for obvious reasons, but Castiel gave Sam and Dean an Enochian warding inscription—he carved it right into their ribs. Unless you've got a high pain tolerance and a really small chisel, I'd move on to the next one.

- **Torment chant.** A line of Enochian that'll wrack an angel's insides with pain. Useful for a hot second, but it won't last. And believe me, you use this on one, they're gonna be pissed, and you'll probably be worse off than if you just tried to run. If you did that, maybe they'd at least take pity on how pathetic you are. Still, the chant is short and it could help in a pinch. The Enochian:

Pizin Noco Iad.

A word to the wise, though—Enochian ain't pronounced like Latin. Get yourself a beginner's guide from an occult shop. Each letter is pronounced as a single syllable, so it takes longer to say than you'd think.

- **Angel exorcism.** Guess I lied, this one's actually Latin. Close enough. This invocation will pull the angel from their vessel (temporarily) and send them back to heaven. Again, the spell isn't even trying to kill 'em, so they'll just come back more pissed than ever. But if you're about to get your ass smote (smited? smitten?) then it's better than nothing. The Latin:

  > *Omnipotentis Dei potestatem invoco . . .*
  > *omnipotentis Dei potestatem invoco . . .*
  > *omnipotentis Dei potestatem invoco . . .*
  > *Domine in caelo.*

- **Summoning.** I've only got half the puzzle pieces on this one. Angels can be summoned by prayer ("Dear Cass, who art in heaven, could ya shag ass down here for a minute and help a fella out? No? That's what I thought."), but that very rarely works. Apparently they got more important things to do in heaven, besides listening to humans gripe about our problems. If you want an audience with an angel, you gotta have something they want, otherwise prepare to wait a long time on bended knee. There *is* another way, but it's complicated. An Enochian sigil is required, along with a bowl of herbs, which you then gotta light on fire. I don't know the shape of the sigil, I don't know the herbs. What I do know is the Enochian phrase that you've gotta say right as you're lighting the whole thing up:

Nirdo Noco Abramg Nazpsad.

And just like that, you've got an inbound angel. I assume you gotta name the angel you want a visit from someplace in the Enochian sigil, otherwise you'll get the whole heavenly host on your ass, which doesn't sound like a party I want to go to. Those guys could make an orgy somber.

- **Location ritual.** Say you tried the summoning ritual and it didn't work. Your next best bet: tracking down the angel and going to them. Here's how. Take a clay bowl, inscribed with this sigil:

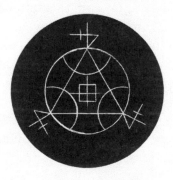

1. In the bowl, place two chunks of conse-
   crated bread (or Communion wafers), the
   wing bones of a bird (don't matter what
   type, as long as it flies), and the following
   herbs:

   > Marjoram
   > Coriander
   > Cumin
   > Mustard Seed
   > Rosemary

2. Or, if you're lazy, just use Mrs. Dash sea-
   soning, it's got all of those in it. I'm totally
   serious. Check the label.

3. Anyway, take all those, add a bit of holy
   oil (available at fine purveyors of occult
   items worldwide) and light that sucker up.
   As it burns, say the following:

   > Zamran Ils Soba Vpaah Zixlai Groeb.

4. Finally, drop a map into the flame. It'll burn
   away everywhere the angel ain't. Don't be
   surprised if the whole thing disappears—
   unless you've got your hands on a map of
   heaven, the location ritual will only work
   if the angel's on the terrestrial plane.

That's it for the Enochian. I'm sure there's a whole
lot more, but I'm new to angel lore. Learning as I go.
Far as other angel weaknesses go:

- **The Colt.** Only archangels are invulnerable to the Colt's bullets, so that means the rank-and-file are fair game. 'Course, you'll have to find the Colt first. . . .

- **Holy oil.** Maybe I shoulda listed this first, since it's the only real weapon a regular schmuck has against an angel. Holy oil, when lit on fire, can be used to contain an angel like a devil's trap. If they cross a line of burning holy oil, the angel burns. Dead. Gone, forever, not just sent back to heaven. They also can't zap away, and their powers are limited within the circle. You can also make yourself a holy oil Molotov cocktail by taking a glass bottle, filling it halfway with the oil, then stuffing it with an oil-soaked rag. Light the rag on fire and throw, but be warned—if you miss, you're as good as dead.

What am I leaving out? My eyes feel like they're gonna fall out if I don't get sleep soon, but my mind won't ease off the gas. So much I've gotta get written down. I could go on with angel stories forever, especially if you count all the ones about Gabriel, who for the longest time we thought was a trickster named Loki—wait. Trickster. Messy workmanship, godlike power, sketchy motivation . . .

I need to go back to the junkyard.

ANANSESEM

DIDN'T FIND WHAT I WAS looking for in the junkyard. I was hoping—well, kind of hoping, anyway—that I'd find candy wrappers. See, Gabriel has a sweet tooth, and leaving candy wrappers behind was always his trademark. The guy ate more Reese's Pieces than E.T. Not that this could actually *be* Gabriel, since he's dead—Lucifer shanked him like a . . . thing you shank. Though it wouldn't be the first time that a piece was put back on the chess board after it was knocked off— God (or whoever's up there pulling strings) has been known to bring back people He's taken a shine to. Like Cass, twice, or Sam and Dean, a bazillion times.

Either way, there's no sign of Gabriel by the Chevelle, but that doesn't mean one of his ilk isn't involved here. By that, I mean *tricksters*, the wiliest bastards ever to walk the planet. Like I said, their power borders on godlike, and they're petty, vindictive, sometimes arbitrary with their victims—they're creatures whose sole motivation seems to be teaching people stupid lessons.

You know what? Speaking of stupid lessons, I think this'd be a good time for a little mental exercise. A "what would you do?" activity, to see if you've learned anything yet. Because Lord knows, I didn't make the right calls when I was in this situation.

Years back, must have been the late eighties, I was on a solo hunt in the backwoods of Arkansas. It was hotter than Hades, and muggy, too—not my ideal vacation spot. I was looking into the deaths of five elderly women from a nursing home outside Calico Rock, all of whom died in fires. Separate, self-contained fires, all within the walls of the nursing home. Now, fires by themselves aren't mysterious, but in each case, the fire marshal's report stated that the fire's source was on the women's clothing. No accelerants were found at the scenes, but the fires burned rapidly and uncontrollably, until they suddenly stopped. As if all the air had been sucked out of the room. Always after the woman had been totally consumed by the flames. Starting to sound like my kind of work, right?

My investigation was by the book—interviewed witnesses, nobody saw anything. Interviewed family, learned that the women knew each other, mostly from their bridge games at the home. Calico Rock isn't a big town, and they'd all lived nearby their entire lives, so they were bound to have run into each other over the years, but everyone remembered them as nice ladies who largely kept to themselves. Gossiped a bit, but who doesn't?

My working theory: ever heard of spontaneous human combustion? Each woman had been im-
molated entirely without burning down the rest of
the building. No heat sources were nearby. Nobody
saw anything out of the ordinary—just a sudden fire
that went out just as suddenly. Nothing else seemed
to fit. The question became: why? Who (or what) was
behind it?

The only person to say anything out of turn about
the charbroiled women was an old widower who
lived in their nursing home. He had skin the color of
burned toast, and a smile that made him seem less
than trustworthy, but any source was better than
none. He told me that the old women argued over
their bridge game constantly. That, at the end of the
day, they couldn't stand each other, but had no one
else to talk to. Said they'd been friends so long they
knew exactly what was most annoying and infuriating about each other. An interesting wrinkle, but
not solid enough to base any conclusions on. I looked
through their few possessions—they weren't dab-
bling in black magic, they hadn't made any demon
deals, they weren't suicidal arsonists.

I spent a week in town, poring over every scrap
of intel, over and over again. Thinking I must have
missed something. That's when I found something—
names.

Jeremy Prious
Alberta Prious
Maybelle Prious

The same names appeared in the wills of two of the deceased women. A connection that nobody had mentioned. When I asked after the names, the families of both women dismissed the connection. A woman named Georgiana Prious had been a housekeeper in Calico Rock, and those were her children (now grown). Georgiana had worked for both families, and it was out of gratitude for her hard work that money from each estate was set aside to make sure her children got an education—only those children were thirty-six, thirty-three, and twenty-eight, so the story didn't hold up. "My mother hasn't updated her will since my father passed," one girl told me. "That must be why the Prious kids are still listed." Bullshit. Something was up, and I was going to get right to the bottom of it.

I went through the newspaper microfiche at the public library, searching for any mention of Georgiana Prious. As a housekeeper in the fifties, she didn't come up much. The part I haven't mentioned yet—Calico Rock was something like 97 percent white, and the Prious family was African-American. I try to keep my head above any of that sort of racial nonsense, but it seemed like it could be a factor in whatever had happened.

After hours of fruitless, mind-numbing searching, I found the one and only mention of Georgiana Prious in the public record—her obituary. March 19, 1964. *Died in a fire*. There *was* a connection here, but not enough information in the article to let me piece it together.

Looked into the other three women's wills—none of them had any reference to the Prious family, but I didn't stop there. I went back to their next of kin and asked about Georgiana, and all of them knew who she was. She'd only worked for one of them, but another had heard about Georgiana's tragic death, and the last one—a Mrs. Baldwin—well, it was her house that Georgiana died in. While, according to the police, Prious was *robbing* the Baldwins. The fire was electrical—an accident—and Georgiana was trapped inside the basement to burn while the fire department tried to put out the blaze.

It was time to talk to Jeremy, Alberta, and Maybelle Prious.

Getting the three of them into one room was a trickier proposition than I imagined it would be—they all hated each other, and hadn't spoken in almost ten years. The only way I could convince them to meet was by dangling the carrot of a payout from the estates of the fried-to-a-crisp women. When they heard the amount they were entitled to, they reluctantly agreed to join me at the local watering hole for a drink and a quick chat.

What followed was the most uncomfortable first drink I've ever had, followed by a few so-so drinks, then a revelatory fifth through eighth drink. The Prious kids were beyond damaged by what had happened to their mother. She was the woman who took care of them, the only person they had in the world (their father had been killed in an automobile accident when the kids were young), and she died tragically, only to be afterwards accused of a crime they knew she didn't commit. Their mother wasn't a thief, she couldn't have been one—she had three kids to support, she wouldn't risk being arrested or losing her housekeeping jobs.

It was more than that, though. The kids believed that Georgiana was the victim of a cover-up—that the police knew that she wasn't robbing the house, but was an invited guest. For what reason, none of them could even venture a guess. All they knew was that all of the women who had died—they had all been close friends at the time of Georgiana's death, and they all had conspired to keep the circumstances of her passing secret.

What Jeremy, Alberta, and Maybelle did about their mother's death in the years that followed, that's what drove them apart. Jeremy ended up spending a year in juvenile detention for grand theft when he was fourteen years old. That got him separated from his sisters, put into a different foster home that was equipped to deal with "problem children." Maybelle was furious. Jeremy stealing just made their mother look guiltier. Maybelle wanted to go through the proper channels to get justice—sue the town for malfeasance and for libel against her mother, but couldn't get anyone to help her take the case to court. Hard for a broke teenager to get anything done, especially when she's an orphan. She banged that drum until no one would have anything to do with any of the Prious kids, made things even more difficult for all of them. And Alberta . . . when she was sixteen, she dropped out of school and went to work as a housekeeper. For the Greysons—one of the families that Georgiana had worked for. One of the families that Maybelle and Jeremy were sure had been involved in covering up their mother's death. Maybelle couldn't stand it. She started rumors about her sister, saying that she was sleeping with the man of the Greyson house. Mister Greyson had no choice but to fire Alberta, and she wound up on the street. It all spiraled out of control, until here we were—drowning our sorrows in whiskey (gin for the ladies) and wondering what really happened all those years ago to Georgiana in that basement. It was the one thing the Prious children still had in common—they wanted the truth.

That's when Alberta said it. "I suppose Mrs. Greyson must be terrified. All of her old friends dying like that." I was so into my cups I hadn't realized it—Greyson wasn't one of the women who'd been killed. She was out there, alive, and quite possibly the next target.

So here's the first quiz—you all know who the most likely suspect is, right? Don't take a genius. Go ahead. Guess.

You said Maybelle, right? Figured that she was

the most irked by the injustice done to her family, couldn't get any results from the legal system, so she started looking into other options, like black magic—maybe hoodoo, maybe something more esoteric. Began to pick off the old ladies who did wrong by Georgiana, one by one.

Wrong.

Maybelle could not abide her brother tarnishing their family name by committing the very crime Georgiana was falsely accused of. No matter how much she wanted to, she would never kill someone—because that'd mean she was just as guilty as the people she wanted to punish. She preferred to suffer on, telling anyone who'd listen about the real facts of the matter. And Jeremy, well, he'd learned a harsh lesson in his youth about the consequences for disobedience. He'd lived his life on the straight and narrow since then. Started a family. Moved on.

Alberta, though . . . her life had been ruined by the tragedy. She knew all of the women involved, knew of their alleged involvement because of her older sister's campaign. Had just as much reason to hate those women as Maybelle and Jeremy. The most important fact, though, is the most human—the one woman who *wasn't* killed was Mrs. Greyson, a woman who had taken Alberta in when she was desperate and given her a home and a job. It wasn't Mrs. Greyson (or even Mr. Greyson) who was responsible for Alberta losing all of that, it was Maybelle. Alberta was my suspect. Revenge the motive. Black magic the means.

Question number two: With all that in mind, what's the next move?

A. Go to Alberta's apartment, ransack the place, looking for grimoires, magical implements, dead cats, all the usual black magic nonsense.
B. Skip that, assume Alberta's guilt, and confront her.
C. Keep looking for more suspects. Talk to Mrs. Greyson.
D. Leave. Let the matter rest, since the damage seemed to already have been done.

Well?

It's a harder choice than it looks like at first glance. It's one of the most important lessons about hunting—emotions, *your* emotions, play a huge role in the decisions you make. Because, me? After talking to the Prious kids? No matter how little evidence they had, I believed 'em. Georgiana was innocent, and those old women were guilty. Didn't matter that I wasn't sure what they were guilty of, something about the look in Maybelle's eyes as she talked about her mom . . . I wanted to walk away. Justice had been served.

You've got to *fight that feeling.* People were dying, and I couldn't say for sure that it was going to stop. I had to keep digging.

Now, that don't mean you should ignore those feelings entirely. My gut told me that Alberta was behind the spontaneous combustions, and that if I confronted her directly, I could end up combusted myself. Can't have that. I also knew that, if I was right, the lynchpin to solving the whole case was with Mrs. Greyson. She was Alberta's emotional tether— the one person who'd been kind to her through everything. If *Greyson* could confront Alberta, we'd be getting somewhere.

After I'd sobered, I went to the Greyson house. She lived alone in the old country home, having survived her husband by many years. Unlike her friends, she was still able to care for herself, but by the looks of the place, that facility was fading quickly. Mold covered one corner of the living room where water had leaked down from an upstairs bathroom—no one had done anything to stop the leak, so the mold glistened with wetness. Like a green tentacle, reaching down from the ceiling to grab at the many small rodents which scurried along the floorboards. It didn't seem to bother Mrs. Greyson, who was sipping tea with honey and murmuring quietly to herself as I asked her questions. I told her I was from the newspaper, writing an article about the fires.

"What do you remember about Georgiana Prious?" I asked.

"Georgie . . . she was a flower. Wilted too soon."

I didn't know what the hell that was supposed to mean, so I pressed on. "Do you remember what happened to her? To Georgie?"

"Of course."

"Will you . . . ya know . . . tell me?"

It was a lot of that. Back and forth, not getting much of anything from her. It wasn't until I brought up the tragic deaths of her friends that Mrs. Greyson really started to talk.

"They all deserved it, one way or another," she said. "Gossips and sneaks, all of them."

"Thought you were friends," I said.

"Were. Were friends. Years ago."

"And now you're not, because of what you did to Georgie?"

She scowled at me, in that way that old ladies are great at. Set down her tea cup. "I didn't lay a hand on her. I took care of her youngest once she was gone. . . . I had no part in that business."

"Bullshit."

Not to say I didn't feel for the woman, but there's a certain art to prodding people into confessions. I could tell that Mrs. Greyson *wanted* to tell me more, but she was censoring herself. Thinking about her responses too much. I needed to get her agitated, make her talk faster, without the filter.

She went through the usual motions, "Who do you think you are?" and "You're a guest in my house" and "In my day . . . ," but none of them convinced me that she wasn't involved in Georgiana's death.

I asked more direct questions, like, "What was Prious doing in that house in the first place?" which she dodged for a while, until, finally—

"She shouldn't have been there. She should've

known that what she was doing was wrong without us telling her."

Behind me, the front door creaked open. Balls. I'd convinced Alberta the night before to join me at Mrs. Greyson's house, but not for another half hour—I wanted time to get to the bottom of things, get Greyson on my side and ready to talk sense into Alberta. I needed at least another five minutes, I was just getting to the good stuff. Except, it wasn't Alberta. I heard the sound of a cane scuffing on the old hardwood floors. The uninvited house guest ambled in, didn't notice me sitting in the dimly lit sitting room until he was right beside me.

It was the widower from the nursing home, with the burned-toast skin. A man who claimed to only know the deceased women because they lived down the hall from him. Suspicious as hell that he'd show up out of the blue.

"Oh," he said. "I'll come back when you don't have company, Mrs. Greyson."

These were the options, as I saw them in that moment:

A. His visit was random, if incredibly coincidental. Let him go and get back to grilling Greyson.
B. He was another piece of the puzzle I didn't yet understand, but Alberta was still the killer. Hold him there, wait for Alberta to arrive, let the sparks fly. Kill whoever seemed appropriate once they got their stories straight.

C. The widower was the real culprit, here to finish
the job. Get him outside, out of Greyson's view,
and kill him.

D. Kill 'em all, let the boys up and downstairs
sort 'em out.

Maybe you're smarter than me. But me, facing
those options . . . like hell I was gonna let him go.
I beat him to the door, closed it. Bolted it. Made
it clear that he wasn't going anywhere, which he
wasn't psyched about. Whether he or Alberta was
the culprit . . . that I didn't know. I had to ask more
questions.

It became clear very quickly that Mrs. Greyson
had no idea who the old widower was, or what he
was doing there. One more strike against the guy.
He claimed innocence, saying that Mrs. Greyson's
memory wasn't what it used to be (happens to the
best of us). That they were fast friends, and that
he had no idea she had a connection to the burned
women. Likely story, buddy.

He claimed his name was Omar Adams, that if
we called any of Mrs. Greyson's friends, they'd back
up his story. I decided to call his bluff, went to the
next room to get the phone—remember, this was the
eighties—with the real intention of getting a knife
from the drawer. I had a gun in my jacket, just in
case, but the situation felt like it was getting away
from me and I wanted to cover my bases. When I
reached for the knife block, Omar's hand was already

on the butcher knife. He hadn't even been in the room a second earlier.

"I thought you were going to make a phone call?" he asked. I noticed that he wasn't holding his cane. He didn't seem to need it.

The doorbell rang. Cut the tension like the knife I now couldn't grab. This time, it *was* Alberta at the door. She'd shown up early after all.

I went to the door, unlatched the dead bolt, now realizing how pointless it had been to lock it in the first place. The widower had teleported himself into the kitchen, I was sure of it. My eyesight ain't perfect, but I know when somebody goes from being not there to there in an instant. What'd that make him? At the time, I didn't think angels existed, certainly didn't know they could teleport. So what? A ghost? Sure didn't look like one.

As Alberta walked into the sitting room, I reached into my jacket, found the cool metal of my pistol. If I was facing a creature that could both teleport and spontaneously combust people, the only advantage I had was that of surprise. I needed to act.

The widower wasn't surprised. Not even a little.

Before I could level the gun on him, I felt my feet lift off the ground, and I was ratcheted backwards, over a chair, into the hall, banging past obstacles on the way. I fired off a shot, but the bullet dug ineffectually into the wooden banister leading up to the second floor. My body slammed into a wall with incredible force, my head swimming from the impact. I

wobbled forward, tried to level the gun once more . . .
and that's when everything went dark.

. . . . .

When I woke up, I felt the warm trickle of blood
down my back. I couldn't see anything—figured I
must have been in the basement. The old house had a
storm cellar that had been sealed up for years, which
I found when doing recon work on the place before
I went inside. Seemed like a discreet place to dump
a body, if need be. Didn't think it was gonna be *my*
body getting dumped.

Across from me, something stirred. Weight shifting in a chair.

"I didn't mean to hurt you," the darkness said.

"Like hell," I said. "Don't toss me through a wall
next time."

"I have a right to defend myself," the voice said.
The widower's.

"What's your real name?" I asked the darkness.

"Anansi," the widower replied, hesitantly.
"Maybe you've heard of me."

I certainly had heard of Anansi. He was a trickster god from West Africa, had made the crossing to
the Americas with a slave ship in the 1700s, if you
believe the legends. Which, of course, I do. He was
a keeper of knowledge in the old world, and was
known for telling stories—they called 'em Spider
Tales, or *Anansesem*. Was famous for playing tricks
on people, teaching 'em lessons. Lore said he took the

form of a massive spider when he wasn't blending in with humans, which seemed about right—there was something about his face that seemed spiderly. I made a remark to that effect, asked why he wasn't out spinning a web.

A match was struck in front of me, the light from it illuminating the crags and valleys of Anansi's face. "Ah, yes. I recognized you as a hunter . . . from your smell. You smell like death, like killing. I thought you'd have recognized *me* sooner," he said, pointing to his face. "My mask isn't very subtle. I'm a *black widow*er." He smiled. The "*Get it*?" was implied.

Why do monsters always gotta make bad puns? I'll never understand it. I moved on. "One of the Prious kids summoned you?"

Anansi laughed. "No, no. No one summons me, anymore. I go where I go, and right now, I'm here."

"Blowing up old ladies."

"Just deserts. The wheel just brought back to them what they put on it." Anansi leaned forward. Squinted his eyes at me. "You don't agree?"

"Can't be sure," I said. "I don't even know what they did."

"They burned a woman alive," he said. "That's bad for your energies. I can smell that, too. Good sense for these things."

I asked him how we was so sure. He laid out the whole story, which he'd gathered from eavesdropping on their bridge games for the last five years—see, Anansi was retired. He'd given up his ways. Taken up life as a human in a nice little retirement home, only to be drawn back into service by the cadre of old women whose secret he overheard.

Georgiana Prious had been dating, in secret, the son of one of the women—a man by the name of Arden Baldwin. Arden had met Prious while at a social function at the home of one of his mother's friends, where Georgiana was employed as a part-time housekeeper. They knew that their relationship wouldn't get a good reaction from the Baldwin family, not because of her race, but because of her position—a servant, more or less. The Baldwin family was wealthy, as far as Arkansas went, and his familial duty as a firstborn son was to marry well and keep the family money in good (already rich) hands.

One day, a group of six women gathered to discuss an upcoming church event—because they were all good Christian women, of course—and came upon the secret relationship between Georgiana and Arden. Mrs. Baldwin was less than tickled by her son's dalliance, and sat him and Georgiana down—forcibly. Neither of them was going anywhere until they agreed to call off their little fling. Problem was, love don't work like that, and neither was receptive to the idea . . . until the family money came into play. Mrs. Baldwin, at the prodding of several of her friends, told Arden in no uncertain terms that he'd be thrown off the gravy train if he didn't renounce his servant girlfriend there and then. But the whole while, Georgiana, who was terrified, of course, was figuring a way to escape. While Arden was weighing his options, Georgiana bolted, and Mrs. Baldwin chased her. I don't have all the details of the next part, but what I do know is that things went from bad to worse. At the end of a scuffle, Mrs. Baldwin was standing over the unconscious body of Georgiana, and a tipped over lamp had sparked a small fire. They had a choice—I'm sure for a rich lady with everything to lose, it seemed like an obvious one. She and her gaggle left the girl inside to burn.

Part I don't get? Why that idjit Arden didn't speak out. I get it was his mother, but still . . . if he loved that girl, he shouldn't have let things get so pearshaped. She had kids, for God's sake.

So there I was, sitting across from Anansi, head still foggy from the earlier violence. The whole story now told. From what I'd heard, it did sound like the women deserved it. I asked him what he was going to do with Mrs. Greyson upstairs.

He sniffed the air, asked me a question: "You can't smell it?"

I could. Smoke. Mrs. Greyson was already dead.

This is where the no-win scenario kicks in. The trickster had already done all the damage he was gonna. He'd killed all six women responsible for Georgiana's death and the cover-up. And in a way, he might have been right to—weren't they the villains in the story?

So I got no idea why I did what I did next, and I

honestly can't say if I'd do the same thing if I was in the same position now. . . .

I leaned far forwards, put my head in my left hand, like I was overcome by emotion from his story (he was a storyteller, I knew he'd buy it)—and I used my right hand to reach down to my boot, out of Anansi's sight. There, I kept a silver dagger, for occasions just like this. With one swift move, I pulled the dagger from its sheath, swung upwards, and stabbed it into Anansi's lower jaw, so the blade went all the way from his chin to his forehead, the tip splitting out of his skull like one of those sandwich toothpicks.

Anansi spasmed, fell to the side, his eyes wide— that time, he *was* surprised.

I'd love to say I double-checked the lore, stayed behind to clean up the scene, or even checked in on Alberta, whose fate I still don't know. I didn't do any of those things. I ran. I got in my car and got home as soon as I could.

What I didn't know then— it takes a lot more than that to kill a trickster. . . . And there's no reason the thing you're hunting can't follow you home.

THE CRUSHER

BY THE TIME I GOT BACK to Sioux Falls, I regretted my speedy exit from Calico Rock. If there was one thing I'd learned from Rufus, it was that . . . well, I mostly learned how to be an alcoholic from Rufus, but if there was another thing, it was that you can't cut corners. In fact, that was Rufus's #1 rule, but I'll get to the rules later, if I can still remember them.

When I pulled into the salvage yard, I went right inside to my library. I knew I'd read about tricksters in one of my lore books, but I also knew it was gonna be a long night of reading before I tracked the stats down. This was before the Internet, see, and we couldn't just Google the name of the monster and get some occult nerd's website detailing all the ways to gank it. Still had to do things the old-fashioned way, with sleepless nights and paper cuts and the smell of mildewy paper from the old books. Mighta taken longer, but I preferred it that way—which is probably why my house still looks the way it does. If Sam had his druthers, my whole library would be digitized and searchable by now, but that'll happen just as soon as my ass grows wings and flies to Jupiter. I guess flying to Uranus woulda been a funnier joke, but I think there were enough asses in that sentence as it was.

Anyway, I went inside, got right to research. If I ever had the bad luck to run into a trickster again, I was gonna be prepared. The next morning, I finally found the book I was looking for—a giant encyclopedia called *Gods of the African Jungles & Plains*, by a scholar named Michael Cowan who specialized in these things—I met the guy in person last year, found out he had a run-in with a trickster back in the seventies, while on an aid mission to a remote village in what was then Zaire. He took one too many jabs at the smell of the dung huts, offending the trickster. 'Course he didn't know it was a trickster at the time. For all I know, it mighta been Anansi he offended, since there's nothing stopping a demigod from flittin' back and forth across continents whenever he pleases. Anyway, when Michael got back to the States, none of his family recognized him, and I mean not even a little. His son thought he was a home invader when he came in through the kitchen window (his keys didn't seem to work anymore) and almost shot him with his own hunting rifle. Another man was living in his house, driving his car, sleeping with his wife . . . and everybody was acting like he was the crazy one. Eventually, his doppelgänger revealed himself to be the trickster, and demanded penance from Michael. In exchange for returning his life to normal, the trickster wanted Michael to live in a dung hut, like the ones he'd made wise cracks about in the village he'd visited in Zaire. Facing that or losing his entire life and everyone in it forever, Michael chose the hut. Still lives in it. For all his belly-aching about it, the hut smells better than you'd think. That's what drove him to compile all of the trickster lore, to save others from the same fate. Inside the book, I discovered this:

That's Anansi in his native form—bit uglier than the old widower I'd met the day before, but in a way I could see the resemblance. What I read about him scared the piss outta me—according to lore, a trickster can only be killed with a wooden stake dipped in the blood of its victim, and I certainly hadn't done that to Anansi. Made me wonder—if Michael Cowan researched everything there was to know about tricksters, why hadn't he ever killed the one that'd sentenced him to life in a house made of shit bricks? Probably because of this next bit:

> *If, by some terrible circumstance, one discovers him or herself caught in the vexing iron sights of a trickster (or demigod of similar capacity and deftness for matters of ill-repute), the remedy is not reprisal or violent ends, but rather capitulation. Though their deficiencies are well-documented in tribal stories (primary sources listed in Appendix C), the trickster is not to be trifled with by mankind. They are, by their very nature, impetuous and quick to anger, quick to judge, and quick to smite those whom they believe to be deserving. The justification for their actions may be capricious and without merit, their mannerisms childish. Despite that, never forget that they hold dominion over energies and magicks vastly beyond the limits of human understanding and will use them, frankly, to make your life miserable for the simple reason that they find it humorous.*

Okay, so, maybe you read that and thought, "Guess I'd better steer clear of tricksters," but what I took from it was that I'd better find a pointy stick and the blood of one of those spontaneously combusted grandmas from Calico Rock so that I'd have a fighting chance against Anansi if I ran into him again. That meant turning right around and driving cross-country again, probably breaking into a morgue or digging up a grave, just on the off chance that Anansi doesn't give up his self-imposed retirement. Them's the breaks.

I put some ribs on the barbecue (for courage) and planned out my strategy—I was gonna try to get to Mrs. Greyson's body before it was interred or cremated—if I was too late, the job'd be a whole lot messier. Nobody likes digging up six feet of dirt, much less poking and prodding a mangled corpse. I re-packed my duffel bag full of weapons and other hunting implements and made my way out into the junkyard, where I'd parked.

The sun was setting over the twisted wrecks of cars in the salvage yard—I'd somehow spent the entire day scouring through books without realizing it. Happens more often than I'd like. A wolf's howl caught my attention, coming from the forest behind the yard. Wolves aren't unheard of in South Dakota, but they're uncommon in these parts. Especially back then, before the "Save the Wolves" effort was in full swing. You were more likely to see a farmer standing over the carcass of a wolf he'd just killed than hear a wolf in the wild. Hearing it was odd, but I didn't think anything of it until I heard the exact same howl again only seconds later—and this time it was behind me.

It's a little spooky for *anything* to move that fast, much less a creature with fangs and a taste for bloody red meat, so I decided I should play things safe and pulled a .22-caliber rifle out of my duffel. That kind of firepower would drop a wolf no problem. I got near my car, felt like I was home free . . . then I heard the whimpering. I spun around, fast as I could, scanning the whole yard—I thought it musta been an injured animal, deer, coyote, maybe even a dog, but I couldn't see anything. The critter whimpered again, this time a little deeper, sadder. It was in pain, whatever it was, and it was close.

Enough of this "circle of life" hogwash, I thought, and went back to my business, only to be greeted by the strangest sight as I rounded the car to get to the trunk. A bite was taken out of its ass. I don't mean that metaphorically—something had chomped off the left rear end of the car, slashing into the tire and leaving rent metal with large fang-marks where the bumper, tail lights, and rear quarter-panel had been. *It was the car that was whimpering*. It was friggin' *making noises* like it was a hurt kitten.

Even for me, that crap wasn't normal.

I did the only thing that made sense—I raised my rifle and got ready to shoot it. Hunter rule #27: if a big inanimate object that should never be alive suddenly is alive, you kill it, ASAP. When I got the car in my sights, it growled at me. Deep and guttural, like a bear or a lion. *Great, I pissed it off.*

As I pondered how screwed I was, I realized there was no way a .22 was going to kill something that weighed thousands of pounds. My best options:

A. Run
B. Run
C. Run
D. Piss myself, then run

Then I remembered that it was a car (let's pause for a big WTF here . . . okay, we can continue), and even with one tire popped, it could still outrun me. Outdrive me. Whatever. It could go faster than me, run me down, and squish my head like a grape.

With my rifle still trained on the car, I took a few steps back. My foot ran into the hub cap of a junked old jalopy that'd been sitting in the yard collecting rust for a decade—and the jalopy *barked* at me.

A set of high beams hit me, nearly blinding me. Then another, and another, and another. A dozen engines rumbled to life all over the junkyard. Whatever had happened to my car, it had happened to all of the cars, and none of 'em seemed pleased to see me. In the moment, all I could think was that I shoulda taken better care of them. One of 'em I'd taken all the seats out of, one of 'em didn't have any side panels or doors, one of 'em had been stripped of all its wiring . . . they were going to kill me, and I couldn't help but marvel at how ironic a death that would be, run down by the cars I'd spent my life tearing apart . . . so, of course, it had to be the trickster. Anansi must have followed me home, and was trying to take vengeance on me for what I'd done to him.

If I could have talked with the guy, maybe we could have worked something out. After all, I hadn't successfully killed him, so no harm, no foul, right? What's a little stabbing between friends? I doubted he'd see things that way, but at the time it seemed like it was worth a try. Instead, I tried to plot a course through the pack of rabid junkers between me and my house, but they were moving now; they rolled around on steel rims and bald, flat tires. The sound was terrible—a mix of diesel engine rumblings and the scraping of metal on metal, along with low groans and whispers. The *cars* were *whispering*. Talking to each other, plotting out ways to corner me and kill me and get me back for all the things I'd done to them. I was like a toddler having to answer to his mistreated toys.

Behind me, another wolf-like howl cut above the din of the cars. It was different than the noises that the cars were making—somehow more savage and beastly. Odder than the howl was the cars' reaction to it—several of them flinched back, their reverse lights coming on as they retreated away from the howl. Whatever it was behind me, they were afraid of it, and it seemed reasonable that I should be, too.

At moments like that, you've gotta ask yourself some tough questions, such as:

- Do I have any shot at surviving this? 'Cause if not, you might as well go down swinging.

- What are the chances that this is a dream? I've been trapped in my own dreams before, and things got pretty weird in there, too. In this particular case, it seemed far likelier that this was the twisted workings of Anansi, not my own subconscious (though this *did* seem like something I'd dream).

- Who can I call to get some help? At the time, all the hunters I knew were several states away— this problem was going to be resolved before they'd be able to get to Sioux Falls, one way or the other. Either I'd be a blood stain in a tire track, or I'd— somehow—have found my way out of this.

- What do I do next?

That last one is a bit of a pill, isn't it? Never an easy answer. An army was in front of me, bloodthirsty steel monsters that I didn't understand and couldn't predict. Behind me . . . mystery. Something bigger, fiercer. Angrier?

I chose the mystery. I turned tail and ran as fast as I could, into the darkness at the far end of the salvage yard. At the extreme edge there's a chain-link fence topped with razor wire—don't want anybody sneaking in—that would impede my escape. Luckily, my extracurricular activities meant that I didn't have the time to constantly maintain the fence, and I knew there were at least a couple spots where I could squeeze through a break in the chain. As I got further from the headlights of the cars, I realized that they weren't chasing me. They'd huffed and puffed when I first started to run, but none of them was brave enough to follow. Talking about cowardly cars . . . this still sounds ridiculous, twenty-some years later. But they were. They were alive, and they were chickenshit—scared of whatever it was that prowled the dark end of the lot.

A lot of people, knowing all that, would rather take their chances with the cars than hang out by the mysterious howling beast. After all, the cars were junkers—broken down, some didn't even have engines. Not that their engines mattered much when they were being supernaturally propelled, but they certainly weren't moving as fast as they would have if they were fresh off the dealership asphalt.

This'd be a good time to tell you how my trade works. There's money in scrap metal, more than you'd think there would be. Something like 80 percent of all aluminum that's ever been produced is still in use, 'cause of the magic of recycling and reclamation. Metal doesn't change. It doesn't get weaker with time, it doesn't break easy, it doesn't need to be coddled and babied to last. Sound like anybody you know? People bring me their cars—I buy 'em for cheap, and can make a good living off of selling the bits and pieces back to people that need 'em. Most any wrecked car can still be useful, even if the outside looks like it's been through hell. If only people were that resilient. Now, I told you all that so I could explain the exception—sometimes, a car's been through enough. It's too old, too rusty, too dented to pound back into shape. Every good piece stripped off, sold to the highest bidder. Obsolete to the point that nobody will ever come looking for its parts again. That's a sad thought, right? The day will come when nobody will ever ask about you, ever again. That happens to cars sitting in my junkyard all the time, and when it does . . . they go to the crusher.

The crusher itself is a relic of an older time. I bought it a year after I bought the salvage yard itself, and it didn't work worth a damn. It'd seen too much abuse at the hands of an owner who didn't take good care of it, the gears and inner workings were cracked and corroded, the outside tarnished with the oil of a thousand crushed cars. Their lifeblood stained the machine that had smashed them into an eighteen-inch cube. Took me a year of weekends to fix up the crusher into reasonable shape, and all the while the ancient hulls of forgotten cars lined up to be the first victims of the thing's hydraulic jaws.

Imagine being one of those cars. Being squeezed so hard you collapsed to the width of your bones—it must be like being at the center of the earth. Now imagine that the car crusher suddenly developed a taste for human blood, and it came after *you*—fleshy little bag of meat you. You'd stand no friggin' chance against it. *That is exactly what happened.* I got to the chain-link fence, heard that wolf-like howl, and there it was—the car crusher, come alive, and coming after *me*.

Its massive hydraulic jaws were staring me in the face, gaping open, wide enough to devour me and a Buick at the same time. Red light spilled from the center, as if the crusher had hellfire at its core. I stumbled back, trying to regain my footing as the monstrous thing lifted off its mechanical haunches and started to move towards me. I can't even begin to explain how it was moving, just know that it was in no way natural. It was like pieces of it were coming apart, lifting it off the ground, then disappearing again into the internal workings of the machine as it lowered itself back to the dirt of the junkyard floor. More like a spider than a car. Now, I can't draw worth a damn, wish I could, but here's what it looked like sitting on the ground:

Balls. That didn't turn out right at all. Trust me, it was scary as all hell. The thing had to weigh five tons, easy, and could crush a pick-up truck flat in a few seconds—and now it was alive, howling like a blood-crazed wolf, and chasing me through my junkyard.

Gotta say, this was a low point for me. Not many ways that this could work out in my favor. I ran towards the light from the cars' headlamps, thinking I was better off trying to dodge between several enemies and hope that they obstruct each others' efforts to squash me than go *mano a máquina* with the crusher. I'd seen the power of that thing's jaws, I didn't want that to be me in there, getting turned into a panini.

As I got to the center of the half-circle of murderous cars, I heard the ker-thump of the crusher right behind me as it slammed right through a pile of tires. A second later, a stack of car doors blasted apart as the crusher made short work of them, too. A few errant tires and doors fell into the open maw of the crusher, and it pounded them flat in an instant. Its magical enlivening seemed to have made it even stronger than before, which I was less than psyched about.

The cars began to scatter, which was a small mercy. If they hadn't, I've got no clue what I woulda done—died, I guess. As my Chevelle turned tail, I saw the hole in its backside and realized that the crusher must have done that damage—it was literally taking bites out of cars in the salvage yard. *What the hell was happening? What kind of twisted game was this?* I ducked between two of the cars, both of which lunged at me, crashing their radiator grilles together with a harsh metal clang, missing my ass by barely a foot. Another car, a Pinto, was heading right for me, high beams so bright I couldn't see anything but the oncoming death-mobile. I tried to dodge to the left, but I tripped on the twisted root of a tree I'd dynamited out of the yard when I first bought it. *Shoulda done a better job clearing the roots*, I thought, but there was no time for navel-gazing. I stood up and tore ass for the house, looking back just in time to see the crusher bite down on the car that was chasing me, the grinding of metal on metal mixed with an animal scream as the Pinto was smashed flat. Sparks spit from the crusher's mouth, along with the spray of motor oil and transmission fluid from the car's metal veins.

When you take a car to the crusher, you've already stripped it of every valuable part, and that includes any gas in the tank or oil in the internal workings. As more sparks flew from the crusher's maw, I had a half second to contemplate how dangerous it was to crush a car that still had fuel in its tank before a torrent of flame and shrapnel erupted from the Pinto. A bit of twisted steel sliced into my left calf—I've still got the scar from it. I limped away from the explosion, hoping that it had taken out the crusher as well, but I wasn't that lucky. The giant iron beast emerged out of the fire, blackened from the flame, but still in one piece and as angry as ever. I was only twenty or so yards from my house, but I was starting to understand that my front door wasn't going to be enough to keep the crusher at bay.

I beelined for the back shed, where I hoped to find some kind of weapon that'd put a dent in the beast. I guess the shed isn't really a shed so much as a lean-to, a little working area with a corrugated sheet-metal roof, a shaded spot where I can get some work done without roasting alive in the South Dakota summer heat. Problem was, I didn't have anything bigger than a chain saw in there, and the crusher was at most ten seconds behind me. This was before I got my grenade launcher, see—actually, the crusher is the *reason* I got my grenade launcher. I picked up the chain saw, revved it up, but knew it was pointless. If an exploding Pinto didn't bring the crusher down, nothing in my arsenal was gonna. I had maybe five seconds left.

Let's review what I knew about my situation:

- I'd recently pissed off a trickster, a being of god-like power with a short fuse.

- I seemed to be suffering from karmic payback for all of the bad things I'd done to the cars in my salvage yard, which to me sounds a lot like "just deserts," which lines up with trickster MO.

- Tricksters like to kill people in innovative, out-of-the-ordinary ways, and this fit. Or at least it would, once the crusher ground me into paste.

• Now I had like two seconds left.

So here's the real lesson:

There are times when you're just too screwed to keep fighting. The odds against you are too great, the monster you're fightin' too big and toothy (that's specific to my line of work; your mileage may vary). But with one second left on my clock, I hadn't given up yet. Screw the odds.

I flat-out leaped clear of the lean-to, which shattered into a million pieces when the crusher hit it. The sound of rending metal and splintering wood filled my ears as I rolled clear, and saw what I was after. A two-by-four. Not what you were expecting?

I was fighting a *trickster*, and even if it was manifesting itself as a giant lumbering industrial compressor, it still had to follow its own rules—*Anansi's* rules. After all, the crusher was moving like a spider—if Anansi had taken on the form of anything in the yard, it was the crusher.

Trickster lore: Can be killed with a stake dipped in the blood of one of its victims.

That's all I needed to know. What was a two-by-four but a giant wooden stake?

As for the blood of the trickster's victim—I was losing blood fast out of the cut on my leg, but I wasn't dead yet. I only had one chance at killing the thing, and I wasn't sure how literally "victim" had to be taken for the trickster's vulnerability to work. Across the salvage yard, the flattened wreck of the Pinto was still smoldering where the crusher had dropped it. What was left of it, anyway. I could hear the crusher chewing through obstacles as it chased me, but I didn't turn back. If it was going to catch me before I got to the Pinto, I'd rather not know about it till it was too late. This was a Hail Mary situation, and I wasn't going to get another shot.

Motor oil was pooling beneath the Pinto's mangled hull. I slid to the ground next to it, coating as much of the two-by-four in the stuff as I could, the shuddering *ka-chomp ka-chomp* of the crusher getting closer. If Anansi was going to bring the cars to life only to kill some of them himself, they sure as hell counted as his victims.

Satisfied that I'd coated the board with enough "blood," I turned and was suddenly inside the crusher's jaws. It dug into the ground underneath me, lifting me and a sizable helping of dirt up into the air before starting to chomp down. My equilibrium was thrown off, I had no way of telling which way was up and which was down, all I knew was that the world around me was getting smaller, and smaller, and smaller. . . .

Out of the corner of my eye I saw the two-by-four, resting on a pile of earth inside the crusher's compartment. With the whine of the hydraulics straining in my ears, I propped the board between the upper and lower metal crushing plates, hoping against hope that it'd have some effect—but it snapped in half almost immediately. This, *this* is when I was really, truly screwed. For a second, I saw Karen's face. I was ready. A monstrous scream was the last thing I heard, then—

I was sitting in the dirt of the junkyard, and everything was still. Silent. In the distance, I saw the crusher. Inert. Sitting in its corner like it was any other night.

Out of the shadows, a man emerged. Anansi, in the form of the widower from Calico Rock. He was holding his jaw, as if he'd just been socked.

"Bobby Singer," he said. It's never a great sign when the monster knows your name.

"Anansi," I replied, pretty sure I was about to be turned into a tire or a steering wheel or some such trickster malarkey.

"That was clever," he said. "Using the oil. I hadn't thought of that; if the board hadn't broken, I would have been in real trouble."

"And what, you couldn't go through with crushing me?" I asked. "You just gonna talk me to death now?"

What he said next, well, until recently, I would have said I'd never forget it. Now I'm not so sure. He said, "Bobby, I understand you. What you do, someone needs to do it. It's not so different from the job that I do."

"What job is that?"

"Righting wrongs," he said. "Looking after my people, no matter how far the winds have scattered them."

I shook my head at him. Couldn't believe it. "Blowing up old ladies ain't righting a wrong, it's murder. Call the cops next time."

"You tried to murder me," he said, and he kind of had a point. "On the fringes of the world, the only justice is vigilante justice, and hunters have known that for thousands of years. What you *don't* know . . . is that you're not the top of the food chain. Everyone thinks that they're the lion, but somebody has to be the gazelle."

"That make you the lion?" I asked.

He nodded. "One of the lions."

"So what was all this? A lesson?"

"A warning."

Anansi wanted me to keep hunting. He put just about everything back the way it was, minus my leg, which he said I needed to patch up myself. His warning was simple: don't presume that I was the only force out there trying to set things right. And don't for a second forget that there were things in the world that could snap me like a twig.

After Anansi had gone, I looked around the salvage yard, at all the cars, now peacefully resting. His lesson had worked—I'd never think of myself as king of this place again. There's always gonna be something bigger than you, stronger than you. And they're probably closer to you than you think.

AND THEN, I RAN

I WAS JUST OUT THERE AGAIN, looking at the Chevelle's windshield, the word "Karen" scratched into the glass, and it hit me. This could really be it. My last tango, my last hunt, my fuse finally fizzled out. The hour come 'round at last. Maybe all "Karen" means is that I'll be with her soon. Kind of comforting.

There's a reason I didn't tell you the rest of the Karen story earlier. It didn't begin well, and it don't end well, either. It's important, though, the rest of it. . . . It'll tell you who I really am, and that's the whole point of this, right? To get the real story out there, so people don't have the wrong idea about the reasons I did the things I did. Besides, I don't have any other leads at this point, just that one word. Just Karen. So here's how that story ended.

See, after Rufus exorcised the demon from Karen's body, he gave me the starter course, Monster 101. The same starter course I'm giving you, only he didn't spare me from any of the darkest stuff, didn't pull any punches. He told me about things he had seen in the line of duty that made me sick to my stomach, and that was the entry level stuff. Rufus had a purpose behind the grisly info-dump: for whatever reason, he thought I had potential.

Rufus had been tracking the demon across several states, knew its MO, so he was expecting a bloodbath when he got to my house. He had seen omens (which I had seen too, but dismissed as South Dakota weather), and followed them right to my front door. What he found inside didn't match up with his expectations— yeah, there was blood, but it wasn't mine. I hadn't been able to expel the demon, but I'd held my own against her, and I guess Rufus saw something in that. Thought I'd make a decent hunter, if I got the proper training. It just so happened that Rufus was starting to feel a little lonely out on the road, and was looking for an established hunter to partner up with—only most hunters aren't the extroverted sort. Everyone he'd talked to about it had dismissed it out of hand. Training a partner suddenly seemed a hell of a lot easier than recruiting a veteran.

Rufus was different from a lot of hunters—he had a family. He had a girlfriend of sorts in Omaha who he was madly in love with but couldn't stand to be around. He had a daughter with her who was about nine or ten when I first met him. Rufus never married his girlfriend (her choice, not his), but they were as much a family as anybody, just with a few little idiosyncrasies, like he was never home and when he was, he brought home monster heads, not the bacon.

Both his girlfriend and daughter knew what he did, and both of them supported it (as much as you can support your loved one putting themselves in mortal danger on a weekly basis).

Guess he saw a kindred spirit in me, wanted to take me under his wing, but after a few hours of "Story time with Rufus" I'd had enough. I told him in no uncertain terms that I wanted him to go, to leave me with my dead wife and let me grieve. That's when he told me the worst part. Once you know about these things, the hits don't stop coming. The demon had been exorcised, but not killed. It was still out there, and could come back at any time. What's worse, other stuff will start finding you, too. Like there's the smell of crazy on you, all sorts of critters will come out of the woodwork once you've had an experience like that. I know now that he was exaggerating—most people can go back to living their ignorant lives and just pretend that they didn't see the horrible things they saw, but at the time, it was like he was giving me a death sentence. Not only was my wife dead, but there was no way for me to continue my life either. My choices, as he laid them out, were between going to prison for my wife's murder or to take up hunting with him.

I'm not at all proud of this, but I took the third option. I ran.

After Rufus had helped me deal with Karen's body, the blood, and the authorities, I slipped away during the night. I'd packed a duffel bag while Rufus was scrubbing blood off the kitchen floor, and that was all I took with me. I drove west, towards California, which Karen had always wanted to visit. She had family on the East Coast, but hadn't ever seen anything west of the Rocky Mountains. As I crossed over into Colorado, I would've given anything in the world to have her in the passenger seat. To let her see the sun rising over the mountains, the clear blue sky . . . I don't want to get all emotional here, but as I drove, I made a deal with myself. I was going to do whatever I had to do to forget what I'd seen, and to live my life as if I was still the same man that Karen had married. Should've known that wasn't possible.

I hadn't set out with a destination in mind, only the desire to get as far away from Sioux Falls and Rufus as possible. That left me with a lot of options—at each fork in the road, I'd make a split-second decision, right or left, north or south, civilization or farther into the wilds. Mostly the wilds won out. There wasn't much I wanted to say to other people at the time—no one could bring my wife back, so what was the point? I spent a week at a campground in the Rockies, living off of small game (I had a hunting rifle in the car when I left my house) and avoiding the locals. Even that was too close to home. I'd been camping with Karen only a few weeks earlier and the memory wouldn't stop barging into my head, no matter what I tried to distract myself with. Mostly booze, if you're wondering. I had to get farther away, somewhere with no connections to my old life.

It wasn't until I drove up one of the hills overlooking San Francisco that a destination came to mind—a freighter called *Nishigo Maru*, out of Japan, that was docked at the shipping yards. Couldn't get much farther away from South Dakota than the middle of the Pacific Ocean. I'd always wanted to take a steamer ship to someplace exotic; there was something calming about the idea of a long journey like that, nothing but the sea around you, salty wind blowing through your beard. I didn't know word one about ships, but I knew enough about engines to be helpful, so I figured it was worth a shot.

Let me tell you, Rufus was right about one thing— for me at least, there was no escaping the life of a hunter. I'd crossed into the world of the supernatural on a one way bridge, and by the time I thought to turn around, a hundred different freaks and monstrosities had followed me. I may have thought I was running away from it. I wasn't. I was diving right into it.

NISHIGO MARU

NISHIGO MARU'S FIRST MATE WAS A GUY by the name of Yoshiro. I tracked him down at a local dive bar where he was celebrating the freighter's impending launch by getting fall-down drunk. Didn't take much to convince him that I'd be an asset to the crew, especially when he couldn't pay his bar tab and I offered to cover him. I was to report to the ship the next morning to meet with the skipper, who Yoshiro assured me was a very reasonable and understanding man. Without anyplace better to go, I decided to make sure Yoshiro got back to the ship safely so I could meet with the skipper that same night. I was glad I did, since the ship was preparing to leave dock when we arrived. They had been warned by the weather service that a large storm was due near the San Francisco harbor the next day, and their captain wanted to avoid it if at all possible. Yoshiro was the last crew member to return, having missed his curfew by several hours.

For bringing the slobbering drunk back to the

ship, I'd already ingratiated myself with the skipper, but he didn't have need for any extra hands in the engine room. He was sympathetic to my desire to find work, but couldn't afford to take on any more crew. Yoshiro's drunken promise wouldn't be honored. Since I wasn't in great spirits to begin with, that was quite a blow. I stood in the skipper's office, staring at his vast collection of books and charts. I wondered what it must be like to have read that many books, to know so much about the world. Looking back, the captain's library pales in comparison to the one I've got, but at the time it was real impressive.

I left the captain's office with no plan. At some point, I was going to have to get a job. Probably as a mechanic at an auto shop, and since I was running out of money, it'd have to be close by. The thought almost killed me. I couldn't imagine showing up for a nine-to-five job and not having Karen to come home to at the end of the day. Getting out of the country was the only thing that felt right. Once the seed was planted, it was all I could think about—I had to go someplace where nothing would remind me of her. I turned on my heel and barged right back into the skipper's office, laid out my case. Told him that I'd lost everything I'd ever loved, that I was a broken man, the whole sob story. They still didn't have a job for me, he said. I told him I'd buy a seat on the boat if I had to, but like I said, I was almost out of money. I only had my car to trade, but that was enough. Luckily, the skipper was a fan of Chevelles. I handed over the keys and told him where I parked it in the port lot. When *Nishigo Maru* returned from Japan, he'd pick up his new ride. And if I found myself bored, I was welcome to help out in the engine room—but they weren't going to pay me a single yen for my services. That was fine by me; as long as I could eat at the crew mess, I didn't need money.

We left port within the hour, but I didn't feel any relief. From the aft deck, I watched the lights of San Francisco disappear over the darkened horizon, and everything was the same. My wife was still dead.

The next morning, I partook in an absolutely disgusting Japanese breakfast of broiled fish and dried seaweed. Honestly, if I'm gonna eat seaweed, I'd almost prefer it to still be dripping wet. At least the salt water would mask the flavor a bit. After gagging down the food, I took a self-guided tour of the ship and came away impressed. She was a cargo container freighter there must have been hundreds of containers aboard, most of them now empty after dropping their shipment of televisions, game systems, and compact cars in San Fran. They'd reload in Japan and be back in a month.

The crew lived the lives of ancient nomads, going from East to West and bringing the treasures of each across the sea. That's the polite version of the story. The truth is that they may as well have been a band of pirates. Dean Winchester could have taught that lot some manners, and that's saying something. The officers were all right, but the crew had been out at sea too long, and it had turned them into crude, hormonal animals. Any time more than two of them gathered, it was like a seventh-grade boys' locker room. I couldn't imagine how they must have acted when they were at port in Japan, where they knew the language—their English was shoddy enough that I didn't see them getting far with American women, though not for lack of trying, and hey, some women value persistence over manners.

My second night on board *Nishigo Maru*, we ended up smack dab in the middle of the storm that we had left early to avoid. I didn't think I got motion sickness, but just try and hold in your dried seaweed after getting rocked around by thirty-foot swells. While trying to keep from hurling, I noticed that my duffel had fallen off the shelf, spilling out its contents. A few shirts, some boxers, and a small leather pouch that I'd never seen before. I picked it up and noticed markings on its side—a pentagram and some gibberish in a foreign language that I couldn't understand. All I knew for sure was that it wasn't Japanese, which meant it wasn't from *Nishigo Maru*. It must have ended up in my bag before I got on the ship, but when?

I opened the pouch and found several small bones and a collection of herbs inside. Even as a layman, I knew that it reeked of witchcraft, and that meant one thing—Rufus had put it there. He must have found my bag after I packed it and added the hex bag. Not knowing anything about the purpose of the bag, I assumed it must have been used for keeping tabs on someone, locating them or even eavesdropping on them. After what I'd seen in the last few weeks, anything was possible.

Without another thought, I searched my duffel and found a silver dagger and a book of spells, neither of which I had packed. The fact that I didn't find them in my bag until over a week after I had left Sioux Falls should tell you how often I was changing my clothes—it was a dark and smelly time for me, I ain't proud of it.

I took the hex bag, spell book, and dagger to the top deck, where huge waves were crashing over the cargo containers. Yoshiro and a few of the deck hands were lashing lifeboats to the deck, just in case the ship took on water and we had to abandon it. Hundreds of miles from shore, that idea didn't warm my heart, but I had a mission to accomplish. I got as close to the ship's edge as I could without getting swept overboard and threw the magical bullshit into the water.

It felt like there should have been more fanfare to the moment, a trumpet blasting or a burst of light as it hit the water . . . a big splash, at the very least, but there wasn't any of that. The stuff just disappeared into the waves, never to be seen by man again. A small amount of the weight on my shoulders lifted, but the majority remained. Yoshiro and the deck hands looked at me like I was crazy, then went back to their work.

Below deck, I tried to get some sleep, but it was impossible. I couldn't even stay on my bunk with the rolling of the ship in the waves. Instead, I sat, played cards with a deck the room's previous occupant had left behind, and thought about how different my life was now than a week and a half ago. Then I barfed from seasickness. Life ain't pretty.

In the morning, I dreaded going to the mess. More broiled fish and seaweed. As I shoveled a helping onto my plate, the chef appeared from the galley, smiled at me. She was a lady of about 65, which explained why I hadn't seen her fraternizing with the rest of the crew (the savages) the day before. She musta been able to read my expression, because she took my plate and dumped the food. Told me that she'd get me something I'd like better—if she had *anything* else back in that galley, it wouldn't be hard for me to like it more than seaweed.

When she came back, the plate was heaping with scrambled eggs and bacon. The woman was my savior. She spoke a bit of English, so we got to know each other over breakfast. Her name was Keiko, which had a nice ring to it. She'd been on *Nishigo Maru* a few months, but had been at sea her whole life. Her father was a deep sea fisherman, and often took his children out on his extended fishing trips. She was the sort of gal who could really tell a story, and I listened to her talk for hours. With the breakfast rush over, neither of us really had much to do on the ship until lunch, so we compared life stories. I left out the most recent chapter of mine, since I didn't want to be thrown overboard for being a raging lunatic.

That conversation felt like the first human thing that'd happened to me since Karen died. When I went down to the engine room afterwards, I musta gone ten minutes without thinking about how godawful life was.

Yoshiro came to my quarters that night, whiskey on his breath. Probably around two A.M. He told me that men were going to come and ask me some questions, and that I needed to tell them the truth. Not having a clue what he was talking about, I smiled politely and closed the hatch in his face.

Ten minutes later, two burly-looking men opened the hatch without knocking, let themselves in. One of them had a holstered pistol, the other was intimidating enough unarmed. They spoke rapidly to each other in Japanese, which I didn't understand a word of. When they finally turned to me, they narrowed their eyes and spoke like they were talking to a child.

"Where is Tamuro-San?" they barked. Tamuro was the skipper's name. Apparently, they'd gone to his quarters to report on a typhoon warning ahead, but he wasn't there. They'd searched the whole ship, there was no sign of him. Everybody on board knew Yoshiro was too big of a drunk to stage a mutiny, so all eyes were on the foreign guy who just came aboard.

My first reaction—maybe I *had* been the cause of his disappearance. Maybe that demon had burrowed back up from hell or wherever it went and followed me here. Not that I could tell my two muscle-y Japanese interrogators that. I pled my innocence every way I knew how, but they didn't buy it. They didn't have any proof, either, so for the time being I wasn't getting locked in the brig.

Early the next morning, I went to the mess hoping to see a friendly face. Keiko already had my plate of eggs ready. She was like my mother, but, you know, *nice*. I told her what had happened the night before, and she was sympathetic. She suggested I watch my back around the rest of the crew, since they were all fiercely loyal to Tamuro-San. If they thought I was the one who offed him, well, I'd have trouble. As I heard other crew members coming down the corridor towards the mess, I made a discreet exit. No sense starting anything over a plate of eggs. I passed a few of the crew in the hall, and they just nodded at me, warily. Not angry, just suspicious.

Yoshiro, on the other hand, would have killed me if he thought he could get away with it. He was sure I'd repaid the skipper's kindness with violence, and since he was now in command of *Nishigo Maru*, that meant trouble for me. I made a mental note to avoid him, but there's only so many places to hide on a tin can. The next two weeks were going to be rough.

I felt an obligation to look into Tamuro's disappearance. If it *was* related to the demon, I needed to do something about it. Rufus had told me the basics about exorcising a demon, but I'd thrown the book he'd given me overboard. Seemed like a stupid move once I needed it. After searching the ship for traces of sulfur and cold spots, I realized how foolish the whole thing was. More than likely, Tamuro just got drunk and fell off the top deck. Working on a ship like that wears on a person, that was plain as day. I woulda predicted that Yoshiro'd be the one to pull that move, but everybody's got their demons. Well, demons in the metaphorical sense. It's hard to use that phrase when often you mean it literally. When I didn't find any evidence of supernatural involvement, I gave up and spent the rest of the day holed up in my bunk. No use stirring the pot by sticking my nose in the engine room.

I met up with Keiko after dinner, heard more stories about her family. It was calming to hear about someone else's life, especially one that was so different from mine. She knew all of the Japanese folklore about the sea—an extensive topic—and could go on for hours about it. I heard about this mythical sea serpent Ikuchi, which used to harass ships sailing between the Japanese islands. Hadn't been spotted in years, so of course the prevailing wisdom was that it never existed at all—that it was just a myth the fisherman cooked up to pass the long hours at sea. Since my encounter the week before, I was much more willing to accept the existence of the otherwise unbelievable, and that included sea monsters. Ikuchi could still be out there, keeping a low profile, waiting for the day when it was again safe to come to the surface. Or maybe those fisherman just saw a big whale. Either way, it was a welcome diversion.

Though I mighta been content to listen to her prattle on, Keiko wanted to hear my stories, too. In particular, she wanted to know how a guy like me ended up on a Japanese cargo ship thousands of miles from home. I guess you can take the boy out of South Dakota, but you can't take the South Dakota out of the boy. I told her as much as I could stomach, that my wife had been killed and that I couldn't bear to stay in that house any more. I told her how much I loved Karen, how it was hard to imagine myself growing old without her. Funny thing is, "Old" to me then was how old I am now. And now, well . . . hunters don't get old. We all die young. So I guess that means I'm still young.

I could sense that Keiko was uncomfortable with my story—who wouldn't be—but I'm grateful she didn't ask me any hard questions. Some people in her situation would have suspected that I was on the run for less sentimental reasons than what I claimed. Hell, if someone told me the same sob story, I absolutely would assume that they'd killed the wife in question and hopped on the boat to Japan to avoid prosecution. All Keiko wanted to know was whether I thought I'd see Karen again. I told her that I really hoped that I would, but that was all I could say for certain. Little did I know that I'd be seeing Karen again on earth, and that I'd have to go through losing her all over again—that I'd have to *kill* her all over again.

As I was getting ready to turn in for the night, Keiko offered me a swig of some rice wine she had secreted under her bed. It was potent stuff, stronger than whiskey. I don't think you could even legally call it wine, so much as turpentine that gets you drunk, but it was better than being totally sober.

The last thing I wanted to do was tell her about the demon, but when liquor and grief mix, they're a potent combination. Between two and three sheets to the wind, I started talking and didn't stop. I got all the way to my paranoid fear that the demon had followed me onto *Nishigo Maru* before she held up her hand, told me she had to rest.

Back at my bunk, I fell apart. I wasn't even that drunk, but I don't remember much else of that night . . . besides briefly considering going up to the deck and letting a wave take me. It wasn't until I said everything out loud to Keiko that it all became real to me. I couldn't ever go back to being just a mechanic. Whatever I ended up being, it would have to be a whole new me. A Bobby Singer that'd be a stranger to the man I'd been for decades.

Some time in the early morning, the wheel on the hatch spun and the door slammed open. It was those two burly men again, plus Yoshiro. He hadn't shaved and looked like he'd been up all night, which in fact he had. Another crew member was missing, this time from the engine room. The engineer had been manning his post alone when he disappeared, and his absence wasn't noticed until the overheating alarms started to sound on the bridge. With no one at the controls in the engine room, the rotors had been left spinning at maximum thrust for far longer than they were designed. *Nishigo Maru* was dead in the water.

Since I had been interested in an engine room job, I was again the first and only suspect. Things were starting to get real, and I was imagining myself getting tied to the anchor and thrown overboard. Yoshiro went so far as to hit me when I couldn't answer the questions to his satisfaction. I told him everything I could, and hoped that they wouldn't ask Keiko what I'd talked to her about the night before.

When they dragged me to the brig, I was actually relieved. It meant they weren't going to kill me outright, so things were looking up. The brig itself wasn't what I'd envisioned, it was more like a closet than a prison cell, with a small metal gate in the door to allow plates of food to be passed in and out. Because the engines weren't operational, the lights were off in the prison/closet, which made it even more claustrophobic. Yoshiro promised he'd be back later in the day for another round of questioning, so I had that to look forward to.

I sat in silence the whole day, never receiving any of the meals that I felt were implied by the gate in the door. Guess they had bigger fish to fry, since when Yoshiro returned, it was with the news that another sailor had disappeared. Despite me being locked up all day, I was still considered a suspect. They weren't sure exactly *when* the guy had disappeared, so it was possible I'd killed him before I was taken into custody. In Yoshiro's defense, it's not like it woulda been reasonable for him to expect that something supernatural was at play, but at that point I think letting me out of the clink would have been the decent thing to do.

That night, I had another visitor. Keiko. She brought a bowl of noodle soup, which didn't fit through the gate in the door. Instead, she passed the spoon back and forth, letting me get enough in my stomach to stave off the hunger pains. She didn't stay long, but her visit raised my spirits enough to let me get some sleep.

In the morning, Yoshiro returned, this time with a gun. Five more sailors were gone. Yet another was found dead, his throat slit. Whatever witchcraft I was doing from in the cell (closet), he was going to make me stop. I asked him if he thought it was more likely that someone else on the crew had snapped— maybe because of the terrible hours, maybe because of the terrible working conditions, or maybe because of all that friggin' seaweed on the menu. Yoshiro didn't find any of that funny.

Whether I truly believed that theory—that another crew member had snapped and started murdering his coworkers—I don't really remember. It must have been pretty clear that something unnatural was afoot, especially since it was so soon after Karen's death. What I *do* remember is Yoshiro sticking his gun through the metal grate and firing off three rounds, all of them ricocheting around the tiny cell. That I didn't get killed was incredible, that I didn't even get *hit* was both a miracle and a testament to how terrible a shot Yoshiro was.

With his hand still reaching through the grate, clutching the pistol, I put every pound of pressure I could on his wrist. I heard it break with a sickening crack, and the gun fell to the floor of the brig. It wouldn't do me much good on the inside of the cell, but at least Yoshiro wasn't holding it any more. He ran out of there like a chicken with its head cut off, nearly tripping over the raised lip of the hatch.

Yoshiro didn't come around so much after that. From what I heard of the outside, things went from bad to worse on the ship as more and more crew members began to disappear and/or be found murdered. I went three long days without food or water, abandoned to starve in the tiny cell, before finally Keiko returned. She told me that half the crew had disappeared, and that Yoshiro was one of them. No one was in command of the ship, no one was even trying to get the engines fixed. They were all just holed up in various corners with guns, waiting for whatever-it-was to come for them.

My head may have been buried in the sand when I first stepped onto *Nishigo Maru*, but by that point I had fully accepted that something unnatural was happening. If a member of the crew had gone 'round the bend, there would be bodies, or someone would have seen something. I told Keiko as much, and she hesitantly agreed. If I hadn't thrown Rufus's book into the storm, maybe it would have given me some clue what we were facing, and what to do to kill it.

Keiko agreed that we had to try to investigate, so she went about finding the key to my cell. She returned an hour later with no key, but a blowtorch she'd taken from the empty engineering hold. I coached her through its use (it was the same model I had for tearing up cars at the salvage yard) and I was finally free.

We went together through the ship, deck by deck, trying to find any clues as to what was haunting the dark corridors. What we found was a lot of water. Water splashed on the deck, water forming trails through the halls, water pooled in places it had no reason to be. Something wet was moving through the ship. Maybe several somethings. When we got to the mess, we found a contingent of sailors barricaded behind an overturned table, one of them holding a pistol. He fired off a shot as we entered the hall, forcing us to retreat back into the corridor. I had Yoshiro's pistol, but didn't see any point in returning fire. The other humans weren't our enemies, even if they thought they were. At the very least, more humans alive meant more potential victims that the ship's intruder could attack before it got to us, and that helped our chances of survival.

Sticking my head in for the briefest of moments, I tried to talk the sailors down. Told them I was on their side, that we were trying to hunt the thing that was hunting us. They shouted back in Japanese, and whatever they said made Keiko blanch. Mouths like pirates, those guys had. Reasoning with them wasn't going to work, it seemed. As we left, one of them shouted at me in broken English: "Who are you?" Guess they didn't get the memo about the foreigner on board. I tried to explain, but the guy just shouted more Japanese. Then something in English about "not one of us." Not very welcoming to outsiders. We moved on.

Below the engineering compartment was a storage area, which seemed like a decent enough place for something shifty to hide out, so we checked there next. As we entered the cargo hold, I saw something move in the shadows. Like it was slithering. I almost fired my pistol into the darkness, but inside a ship like that bullets ricochet like crazy, so I didn't take the chance. If I saw what we were hunting in the light, I'd take the shot.

Broaching the topic of monster lore with someone is never easy, but it certainly makes the medicine go down easier if you're in the middle of a crazy situation like that. Once bodies have started to pile up, people will believe anything. Since I wasn't familiar with sea folklore, I asked Keiko if there were any stories that fit our current predicament. She shook her head, said she couldn't remember any. Something about the look on her face told me she was lying. I pressed the issue, asked her to tell me more about Ikuchi, that sea creature she'd described a few nights earlier. She hemmed and hawed for a spell, then came clean it wasn't Ikuchi, if Ikuchi was real, he woulda eaten the ship whole.

I asked her if there was another option, and she admitted there was. Her father had told her stories about creatures that come up from the deep and steal away men. They can take on human form when they're above the water, their tails splitting into two legs. They're called Ondines in the lore, but most people call 'em mermaids. But there was no way that was happening here, she said. That was just a story.

I reminded her what I'd told her about Karen. That a lot of things I didn't think were real turned out to be fact. Asked her more about the Ondines, but she didn't know anything other than what her father had told her, and that was half a century ago. If my instinct was right, and we were dealing with a sea creature of some sort, we had to learn more about them. That's when I remembered Tamuro's library. A scholar of the sea, he must have had some books about nautical folklore.

On the way to Tamuro's office, we came across another sailor, this one was only a kid, nineteen years old, max. He was soaking wet, shivering, his hands clenched into a death grip on a handrail. When he saw us, he screamed bloody murder. He'd been through something terrible, and the trauma was still affecting him. We tried to help him up, to bring him with us, but he recoiled from Keiko's touch, stood up and ran down the corridor. After he turned a corner, we heard another scream. I ran after him, gun raised, ready for whatever was around the corner, but when I got there, the hallway was empty. All that was left was a puddle of water and a streak of blood.

At the hatch to Tamuro's office, we paused. Something was moving inside. For a second I wondered if it could be Tamuro himself, if somehow he had survived whatever ordeal had befallen the rest of the ship. Whoever it was, they were hidden behind Tamuro's desk, squirming around too much to really be hiding, but hidden from view nonetheless. Pistol raised, I moved around the desk until I got a good look at the man—it was Yoshiro. He hadn't been taken, he'd simply given up fighting and started drinking instead. I asked him what the hell he was doing in the skipper's office, and he held up a bottle of booze. Tamuro's personal stash, and since he was no longer gonna need it . . .

I helped Yoshiro to his feet, asked him what had happened since we last saw each other (besides him getting sloppy drunk), but before he could answer, his eyes went wide and he fainted. I turned to see what he'd been looking at—Keiko. He'd taken one look at her and collapsed. Now that—that was odd.

Pieces were starting to fit together for me, but I didn't have the whole puzzle. I asked Keiko to look through Tamuro's books for any references to Ondines while I tried to revive Yoshiro. As she searched, I replayed the last few hours in my mind. In the mess hall, the guy had shouted that I wasn't one of them, meaning the crew. What if he hadn't been talking to me? What if he'd meant Keiko? I went back a little further, back to my first meeting with her—no one else had been in the mess, they'd all reported for duty already that morning. The next time I saw her, I'd gone in early and left before anyone else got to breakfast to avoid an incident. Then I'd seen her after hours, again by myself. She'd come to my cell twice, both times by herself. I'd never been in the same room with her and another soul at the same time. Maybe she wasn't a member of *Nishigo Maru*'s crew at all. When the sailor in the hallway and Yoshiro saw her, they both flipped out, as if they recognized her—maybe from when she attacked them? And then there was the lore about mermaids—I'd heard the old fisherman's tales, knew that mermaids were always described as female, at least the ones that came to the surface. There was only one woman on the entire ship, and she was standing right in front of me.

Could Keiko be an Ondine? Could the solution be that simple? What that possibility didn't explain was how she came to be on the ship, and how I found myself in another messed-up situation like this so immediately after the demon possessed Karen. It also didn't explain how people were disappearing while Keiko was with me—was there more than one Ondine onboard? Was it still possible that there was a rational explanation for everything that'd happened?

I had a choice to make, and none of the options were great:

- **Confront Keiko.** Ask her flat-out what she was, if she was responsible for the disappearances. The downside of that was it'd require losing any advantage I had—as far as I could tell, she didn't know that I suspected her, and that's a powerful card to have in your hand. I also didn't know the full Ondine lore—was there a specific method to killing them? I'd learned from Karen that some things can't be killed in the ways you'd think, and I had no reason to think that a simple bullet to the head would drop one.

- **Play dumb.** Keep investigating, try to get more information from her. If she was an Ondine and if she'd actually killed all those people, there must have been some reason she didn't kill me (yet). Who knows, maybe she just liked me. Or maybe she had some other purpose in mind for me, and I was walking right into a trap.

- **Try to lose her.** The ship was big, dark, and mostly empty. On the top deck there were hundreds of cargo containers, any one of which could make for an effective hiding spot if I could get to them without being spotted. Wasn't a very manly solution, but it might be the one that kept me alive the longest. This one also fell apart when I thought about the Ondine lore—from the little Rufus told me, it was clear that some of these critters seem custom-built for hunting humans, with senses of smell and vision that are an order of magnitude better than ours. Ondines could very well be one of those critters, and running would only show Keiko that I knew what was up.

- **Shoot first, ask questions never.** The most brazen option. John or Dean Winchester mighta gone in that direction, but I didn't want to take the risk of killing an old woman without knowing for sure she was the killer.

So what did I do? I waited for Keiko to search the books. If she was the Ondine, she certainly wouldn't give me any intel on how to kill her or her buddies — and if I could actually revive Yoshiro, maybe I could get some answers out of him before he passed out again.

I dragged Yoshiro hastily into the attached bathroom. It wasn't quite big enough for two people, but I could use the sink to splash water on his face. Without smelling salts, I was pretty much relying on my ability to slap and splash Yoshiro awake. I'm not a doctor, see, and had no idea if there was a better way to go about it. The upside was that I got to take out a little of my aggression on the bastard while he was unconscious. Three minutes of slapping later, he was up, groggily looking around the bathroom and talking gibberish in Japanese. I made sure he couldn't see or hear Keiko searching in the next room, positioning him so that the hatch was blocking his view. I caught Keiko sneaking a few glances at him as she searched the bookshelves, but she made no move to keep Yoshiro from talking.

Once he was lucid enough to recognize me, I asked him what had happened. He told me that he thought he'd seen a monster in the room with us. Scaly, dripping wet, with a tail like a fish, teeth like a shark. He told me that he must have had too much to drink, and that it wasn't the first time he'd seen something like that after he'd had too fun of a night. That he'd seen them swimming in the ocean a few times, but nobody else could ever see them, and he always realized how stupid it seemed as soon as he sobered up. I told him to rest, stay lying down while I went to get help. Moving over to where Keiko was searching, I found her looking through an ancient text. Must have been at least two hundred years old. She had the book flipped to this page: ━━━━━━━━▶

It was an Ondine, and pretty much matched what Yoshiro said he had seen. I looked Keiko in the eye, searching for any hint that she could be the very monster I was hunting. Her eyes blinked, then she nodded, as if she knew exactly what I was thinking.

"It's you," I said.

"Yes," she answered, softly, so Yoshiro couldn't hear. "I tried to tell you, that night in my quarters. But you weren't ready to see my true face."

"Why are you doing this?" I asked.

Every monster has a reason to do what they do, that's something you'll learn quick when hunting. Maybe they're hungry, maybe they're trying to right

some injustice, maybe they get some kind of sick amusement out of it. But it's never boredom. Keiko, she was no different. She had a family to support. She was the matriarch of an Ondine clan, and they were starving. Humans had poisoned their habitats, fished their territories to extinction. The Ondine population had been dwindling for decades, and they blamed us for it.

But why this ship? Why now? Because of *me*. I'd thrown that damn hex bag overboard, might as well have thrown a giant bag of Ondine catnip into the water. Here's your next lesson—just cause something's magic don't mean it only does one thing. The same mix of odds and ends that Rufus intended to keep demons away drew the Ondines straight to me. And now that they found us, they weren't going to leave until their whole family was well fed.

It was pretty shocking for her to just come out and admit it, and her candor made one thing abundantly clear—she wasn't afraid of me. She knew that I couldn't stop her from what she was doing, so there was no harm in telling me about it.

I was only half right about her reason for not killing me, though—Ondines, as I learned from Keiko, can read human emotions. They're incredibly empathetic creatures, and can literally feel our feelings. When Keiko met me, she sensed my sorrow and . . . I don't know, musta felt sorry for me. What I know now is that Ondine women (who are generally the ones who come to the surface, though the men do come up on hunting expeditions) abhor men with cheating hearts. Ondine males are emphatically loyal and monogamous. The idea that someone would betray their beloved is infuriating to an Ondine. Most of the *Nishigo Maru* crew fit that bill, after spending long years away from their wives and girlfriends. I was the exact opposite. My wife had died and it ruined me. Every second I struggled to even go on, much less chase the next piece of tail that I ran into. To an Ondine woman, I was the perfect man.

That didn't do me any damn good, though. She was still gonna throw the rest of the crew off the boat and let her school of mermen tear them to shreds. I told her that I couldn't let her, but she made things clear—I couldn't stop them. Even if I killed her, there were others already onboard, and I'd never be able to pick them out from the rest of the crew.

Was she gonna let me live? Figuring that out was pretty high on my list of priorities, but she didn't give me a straight answer. Only thing she said: "I wouldn't let you drown."

As I watched, she went to the bathroom and found Yoshiro. He let out a muffled scream, then fell silent. I just sat there, stupefied. Like I couldn't move my own legs (a feeling that I'd get a lot more familiar with later in life). A second later, she dragged Yoshiro's unconscious body out of the bathroom, towards the hatch.

"Follow me. I'll take you to the others."

If anyone ever tells you that, don't do it. Just don't. It never works out.

That being said, of course I followed her. I didn't know what else to do. Before I went, I tore the Ondine drawing out of the book, stuffed it in my pocket. There was some text in Japanese beneath it, but at the time I couldn't read it, so who knows what I was thinking. Better to have it than leave it, I guess. I also made the impulsive decision to open Tamuro's desk drawer, where I found the keys to my Chevelle. Since he had already been taken underwater to be chomped by the Little Mermaid, I figured he didn't need them.

Keiko took me towards the top deck, dragging Yoshiro the whole way. I had a dozen opportunities to try to take her down, didn't act on one of them. It was my first test as a hunter, and I was failing miserably. Fear combined with the logical realization that I had no idea how to kill her combined to produce inaction. In the back of my head, a voice was screaming *she's gonna kill him. She's gonna throw him to the (metaphorical) sharks*. My pistol was shoved into my belt, ready and waiting, but I couldn't bring myself to use it.

Maybe if Keiko had been a man, I would have felt differently about it, I don't know. I tried to tell myself that it didn't matter, that a human is a human, but there's something about shooting a grandma that takes the gusto out of my trigger finger.

When we got to the deck at a little past midnight, several other crew members were already there, tied up, waiting to be thrown overboard. There were gags in their mouths, but I could hear them trying to scream when they saw Keiko. It was then that it really struck me—the old lady in front of me was a monster. Appearances can be very deceiving, and I had to get over that quickly, or all of those men would die.

"What are you going to do to me?" I asked.

She turned to me, smiled. "Same as we did to Tamuro-San," she replied. "He's a good man."

"Was a good man," I corrected.

She shook her head, pointed to the rolling ocean below us.

I looked over the railing and into the sea, where black waves crashed against the motionless hull of *Nishigo Maru*. In the water were several figures—at first I thought they were dolphins, but as I looked closer, they were clearly men. Men with tails. Ondines. He was hard to make out, but I recognized Tamuro's face among them. Waiting for their supper.

Here's another lesson about monster MO: they're *always* trying to turn you. It's never good enough to just live out your life as a monster, you have to make other people join you. Vamps, werewolves, a bunch more, all the same way. Bastards. Ariel might be a good-looking broad, but I had no intention of eating kelp for breakfast, lunch, and dinner the rest of my life.

Tamuro had been turned, and apparently I was next. That was my cue to start fighting back. My new problem was that there were other Ondines on the ship, but they weren't on the deck where Keiko was expecting them. Even if I killed Keiko, I'd never be able to recognize the others, and they'd be a lot less friendly to me once I killed their matriarch. Either way, I still had to make my move before she started tossing guys in the drink.

Keiko dragged Yoshiro to the railing, hoisted him above it with far more strength than you'd expect from a lady her age (or even a man my age), and I fired. Two shots, right in her back. She teetered forward, looked like she might collapse, then hurled Yoshiro into the water. He hit with a splash and was immediately set upon by the Ondines. When Keiko turned around to face me, it wasn't rage on her face, it was sadness. Regret. Like she was bummed out that she was gonna have to kill me.

Needless to say, the bullets didn't kill her, but they did get her attention. Instead of tossing the sailors into the briny deep, she came after me. I ducked through an open hatch and tried to get as much distance as I could from her, but within a few seconds I heard the clank-clank-clank of shoes on steel deck plating.

Turns out, Ondines aren't as great at hunting as I feared they'd be. After I slipped into the radar control room on C Deck, I heard Keiko walk past the hatch and continue down the hall. For a few minutes, I was safe.

I used the time to think of a strategy. How would I identify the Ondines, and then how would I gank them? Listing off all the dumb ideas I had would be a waste of my time and yours, not to mention the paper this is printed on. The eureka moment came when I found myself wishing I had some Kentucky whiskey to settle my nerves—and I remembered what Yoshiro had said. That he'd see things—creatures—swimming in the water on their cross-Pacific route when he was drunk. And that, when he saw Keiko's face, he saw the face of a monster, not an old lady.

Everybody knows that the legends of mermaids

began when a bunch of drunken sailors saw manatees and dolphins in the ocean and, being lecherous and overworked, thought they looked an awful lot like women with fish-parts (*sexy* women with fish-parts). What if, and this was a big if, they weren't hallucinating because they were drunk? What if they were seeing the *truth* because they were drunk? There are creatures out there, like wraiths, that can only be seen in their true forms through a mirror. You see 'em walking down the street, they look like a normal human. See their reflection and it's a hideous, snarling beast. What if Ondines were the same way, but you had to be drunk to see them for what they really are?

I'd been close to drunk with Keiko a few nights prior, but was able to hold myself together. That musta been what she meant when she said, "*I tried to tell you, that night in my quarters. But you weren't ready to see my true face.*" I needed to get *really, really drunk.*

Under normal circumstances, that would sound like the best hunt ever. But this was my *first* hunt, and getting plastered seemed like it could only make my job harder (this was before I realized that whiskey is a hunter's best friend in all circumstances).

Assuming I found some booze and was able to track the Ondines down, there was still the matter of killing them. Bullets didn't seem to do squat against them. I had an idea about that as well— they were basically fish, right? Fish that could flop around on land for a bit, but they were creatures of the sea, na-tively. Take a fish out of water for long enough, they'll suffocate. All I had to do was trap the Ondines some-where where they couldn't get free or have access to water, and keep them there until they dried out. It was only a theory, but it was the only theory I had.

Finding booze on a freighter is surprisingly simple. The very first crew quarters I stumbled upon was amply stocked, and fifteen minutes later I was drunk as a skunk. I stumbled into the hallway, ready to shoot anything with gills. A few minutes later, I ran into a member of the crew—the first test of my theory. The guy's face was swimming around in my blurred vision, but he remained human. He screamed some crap at me in Japanese, but I was too drunk to catch any of it, so I moved on with my life.

Then I saw him. A male Ondine, and boy was my theory correct. His body seemed mostly human, but his image was wavering, coming in and out of focus, parts of his skin morphing into scales and fins while other parts stayed human. I was so intrigued by his appearance that it took me a second to start shooting.

Again, the bullets didn't have much effect, but they did piss him off, and that was all I really needed. The merman chased me up the stairwell onto the top deck of the ship, where the night wind was whip-ping the waves into huge swells. Water crashed onto the deck as I threaded my way through the massive steel cargo containers. Each one was forty-eight feet long, eight feet high and eight feet wide. The value of all the cargo on *Nishigo Maru* must have been in the millions of dollars, but I couldn't be bothered to think about that.

With the Ondine following close behind me, I ducked into one of the cargo containers. On my first day aboard the ship, I'd toured the top deck, noticed that a few of the containers had their steel doors sitting open and had some of their contents removed. I suspected at the time that Yoshiro or one of the other officers had let the crew pilfer through the containers as a sort of bounty, since in the grand scheme of things, a few missing electronics wasn't a big deal compared to the value of the hundreds of containers.

When the Ondine found me in the container, I was ready. Before the bastard knew what was happening, I'd knocked him on his ass (and I was drunk off *my* ass, remember, so it was doubly impressive) and swung the steel door shut, trapping him (and a crapload of Walkmen, probably) in the container. One down, at least one more to go.

I wanted to find Keiko next. Wanted to get it over with. The only place I could think to look for her was the mess hall, so that's where I went. The sailors we had seen holed up there earlier were now gone, a blood stain on the floor the only evidence that they'd once been encamped there. I searched the galley warily, ready for an Ondine to jump out at me at any second. Instead, I found a trail of water leading out of the galley and down a ladder to the lower deck. There, I witnessed a disturbing sight—an Ondine hovering over the dead body of one of the crew. I fired a few shots, but was quickly out of rounds. It was enough to get the Ondine's attention, and soon I had another prisoner locked into a cargo container.

As I checked the steel latch, I heard an inhuman growl next to me. Keiko. Seeing her true face was shocking, but it galvanized my will. I had to kill her, to stop her from hurting anyone else.

Without any bullets, it came down to raw strength. Most supernatural creatures are far more physically powerful than they look, and Ondines are no exception. I tried the same trick that'd worked on the other Ondines, but she moved too quickly. I couldn't trap her. A blow from her hand sent me flying across the deck, smashed my head into a bulkhead. Blood dripped down my face, and all I could see was red. My vision was already swimming from the booze, so it'd gone from bad to terrible.

She kicked me in the stomach, blew the air out of my lungs. Felt like I was drowning on dry land. Another kick, this time with even more force. Across the deck, I saw an emergency kit. Inside would be first aid equipment and a flare. I had no idea what effect it would have, but the flare was the only weapon near me. Scrambling across the wet deck, I had just reached the emergency kit when her hand gripped my shoulder, spun me around, and hurled me into another bulkhead.

I couldn't stand. My head was spinning, my legs weren't listening to my brain. Looking up at her, I told her exactly what I thought of her, in salty language I'd picked up from the *Nishigo Maru*'s crew, which I won't repeat in polite company. Then I asked her if she'd mind kissing my ass before she killed me.

"I told you, Bobby, I'm not going to kill you," she said, then leaped at me. Both of us teetered at the ship's edge, but gravity was on her side. I fell backwards, down five stories from where I'd been to the roaring ocean below.

Water filled my lungs as I sank into the black abyss. It wasn't like I thought it'd be; there was nothing peaceful about death—I was choking and gagging and fighting as I drifted further and further down, away from *Nishigo Maru* and away from any hope of surviving.

Then I saw her—Keiko, who'd dived in after me. She transformed before my eyes, no longer appearing as a hybrid, no longer bearing any characteristics of an old human woman, she became one hundred percent Ondine. Her tail flitted back and forth, propelling her with impossible speed towards me. My vision was starting to get fuzzy, to go black around the edges. I knew I was losing consciousness, but my eyes stayed fixed on Keiko. As she approached me, her mouth opened, and a blue light filtered out of it, sending rays of energy through the water all around us. Her face was nearly touching mine, the blue light warming my cheeks. For a second, my head cleared—it was like the light had given me a breath of air. I knew I was being turned, but I couldn't fight it.

I'd already put my whole effort into resisting her, but with water in my lungs, I couldn't resist any longer. I opened my mouth, reached out to her, and—

Tamuro. From behind her, he grappled Keiko, twisted her away from me. She lashed out at him, scratched at his face with her claws. He had been completely transformed as well, but his face was instantly recognizable. As I watched the two of them battle above me, I realized I was still sinking. The breath of air that Keiko's light had given me was enough to get my legs moving again. I kicked as hard and fast as I could, swimming madly for the surface, which, to my alarm, was getting dimmer instead of getting brighter. I could see the massive shadow of *Nishigo Maru*, but it felt like it was drifting farther away from me. The world was going black. I took one last glance downwards, and saw Keiko's limp body disappearing into the endless deep. Tamuro was disappearing with her. He'd saved my life. Saved my human life, anyway.

Then, a shockwave blasted through the water. It felt like I'd been hit by a truck, but I kept swimming, kept fighting for the surface. A Ford pick-up truck drifted slowly past me, sinking, followed by a dozen more. A videocassette, a computer, an electric guitar. All of the ship's cargo had been thrown into the ocean, sinking as I ascended. When I came to the surface, fire was everywhere. An oil slick covered the water, some of it burning, and the great ship *Nishigo Maru* was split down the middle.

I never found out what happened aboard, but I can take a guess. The Ondines, nearly finished with their task, decided to destroy the evidence, to keep humans from asking questions about what had happened to the crew. A little tinkering with the engines, and *bam*. Ship goes down.

Floating on the surface, gasping for breath, I made my way to a wooden plank. It'd been part of a cargo palette, but the cargo had already disappeared into the water. There, I'd wait for ten hours while *Nishigo Maru* slowly sank, waiting for some sort of rescue.

When rescue finally came, I told them the only thing I could. Engine trouble. Explosion. Crew went down with the ship, valiantly trying to keep her afloat. Here's the picture from the front page of the Tokyo newspapers:

I wonder to this day if the two Ondines I trapped in the cargo containers were ever freed, or if they sank in a water-tight coffin to the bottom of their great sea, drying out within inches of a trillion gallons of water. For what they did to those sailors, they deserved it. And Keiko . . . maybe Tamuro killed her. Or maybe she just gave up on me, decided to wait for the next ship to pass by. Maybe she's still out there.

Some day, you'll be given the same choice I had—and I hope you're smart enough to realize it ain't a choice at all. Becoming a monster isn't an option. Tamuro may have been able to retain some of his humanity, for just long enough to save me, but I'd bet anything that if you ran into him today, his time underwater will have changed him. There'd be nothing left of the man I (briefly) knew.

That was my first hunt. I'd love to say it was a success, but you read the story. Everybody died. Some of the monsters (maybe all of them) got away. That happens. But you gotta keep fighting. When the rescue boat hauled me up from the sea, they asked me where I wanted to go.

I said Tokyo. Wasn't ready to go back. Still had too much to learn.

JAPAN

I ARRIVED IN JAPAN a hunter by choice. Running from it wasn't an option, both because I knew that it'd catch up with me eventually, and because I didn't think I could live with myself if I did. There were things out there that hurt, tortured, and killed innocent people, and if I didn't step up to do something about it, who would? I've never been the type to let my problems fall at other people's feet, and this was no exception. If there were monsters to kill, I was going to be the one to kill them.

Inconveniently enough, I had that epiphany 5,929 miles from the only hunter I'd ever met. Japan had its own share of things that went bump in the night, though, a fact which I'd learned very clearly aboard *Nishigo Maru*. It seemed like a good idea to try to make the most of my time in Japan by learning about the local customs, the language, and most of all, the local hunters.

Picture yourself in a foreign city. A place that you've read about but never visited, and you don't know the language. Imagine you want to find a place to eat or a bathroom or a taxi cab. Those are all difficult but surmountable challenges. Now imagine you want to find the local chapter of a secret organization of monster hunters whose very existence would send shockwaves through the populace if they were ever revealed. Slightly trickier, but as with anything, there are ways.

Here's how I did it. This particular trick works anywhere, because it relies on a simple principle: if two people are after the same thing, they're bound to run into each other eventually. After finding a place to stay and a job fixing American cars to pay the rent, I spent my nights hunting. I did all the research I could at the local library, but the language barrier was steep. There's something to be said for total immersion, though, and within a month I was able to get by in most situations. "Most situations" doesn't cover researching ancient folklore, and I had to ask for a lot of help from the librarians, all of whom thought I was a total nut. Comes with the territory.

Sooner or later, if I kept following up on omens and clues, I'd find a legit monster case. When I did, hopefully I'd run into another hunter, and I'd be on my way. Whether they'd take me into their fold or kill me on the spot, that I didn't know. Rufus had told me that there were hunters on every continent (apparently Antarctica has a bit of a Yeti infestation), but not how many, where they were, or their disposition towards strangers who wanted to learn the trade.

I scoured the Japanese newspapers each morning,

hoping to see signs of dry lightning, cattle mutilation, black smoke, anything that'd point me towards a demon possession. What I didn't know was anything about the local critters, so at first I had no clue what to look for. After a few particularly enlightening newspaper translation sessions with a very wary librarian, I found my first case. Three women had been murdered in the mountainous outskirts of Tokyo, drained of most of their blood, their hearts ripped out. Didn't need any omens for that one, it was obvious that something was amiss. The press was blaming a serial killer, but the police thought a wild animal might somehow be responsible. They hadn't found any fingerprints, DNA evidence, or clothing fibers at the scene, but they did find fur. Animal fur of a type their experts couldn't identify. I learned all that by visiting the police prefecture for that district, posing as a visiting American novelist interested in the case. I may have slightly implied that I was Stephen King, but it was their own damn fault for thinking all Americans looked alike.

Huh. I guess that was the first time I pretexted for a case, something that's like second nature now. At the time it was terrifying. I was sure they'd catch me in a lie, or ask for credentials (so always have a set or two handy), or even arrest me flat-out. None of that happened, and I learned a valuable lesson—if you walk tall enough, speak confidently enough, and have a surly attitude, people will believe anything you say.

My next stop was the house of the first victim.

She'd been killed while watching television, a wacky game show where you had to wrestle members of your family for the right to not get dunked in a pool full of goo. Japan, man, they know how to make good TV.

Nothing seemed off about the gal's family life, and according to her boyfriend, she didn't have any enemies. She was what the Japanese now call *otaku*—obsessed with pop culture. Her bedroom was downright nuts—action figures lined every shelf of the place, posters covered the walls, a few of them a little risqué. To be honest, I really liked the lady. Too bad she was dead.

The police had combed the place well, taken away any clues long before I got there. That's an important thing for you to learn: Get there first.

The police don't know how to handle a vampire case, or a ghost case, or a shifter case, and they never will. That's what your job is, and if you're gonna do it right, you have to get to the scene before it's been wiped clean by the CSI team and before the witnesses and the victims' families have already been questioned five times. Trust me, they don't like having to repeat the same answers over and over again, and you'll get much better results if you are the first one to ask them a question. Also, if they're still overwhelmed by grief, people are apt to slip up and tell you things they don't mean to—clues that can be vital to solving the case.

That lesson learned, I next went to the most recent crime scene—a jogger in a public park had been torn apart with no witnesses. The police were still at the scene, marking out blood spray patterns and trying to determine the weapon that could have been used on the dead woman. Their conclusion—fangs. It didn't seem like any blade could have caused the lacerations that they were finding on the victim's body, but the wounds were too precise to have been caused by a wolf. Wolves were once common in that part of Japan, but had been pushed out of the area by the expansion of Tokyo and its metro area in the last hundred years.

That got me thinking about something Rufus told me. Werewolves, which I was most familiar with because of those old Universal *Wolf Man* movies, were apparently real. They transform from human to beast on the full moon (though you should know that in the past year, we've seen werewolves shifting on the half-moon as well . . . it's all tied into this "mother of all monsters"/purgatory crap that I'll get into later, if I'm still alive). They also are known to kill humans for food, though at the time I couldn't remember if they ate the hearts (they do, that's their main MO).

If it was a werewolf, the relevant facts are these (I didn't know all this when I was in Japan, but I don't have the time left to tell you how I learned it all):

- They munch on human hearts like they're made of candy.

- Their transformation isn't under their physical control. Once they start transforming, there's nothing they can do to stop it.

- They're not like the Hulk. Getting them mad won't force them to turn, but the feelings of their human side will target who they attack when they wolf out. Sam likes to say that they're "pure id," and that whoever they hate as a human is who they attack as a wolf. Best not to piss them off in either human or wolf form.

- They often don't remember anything they do while in their wolfed-out form. That means that some of them don't even realize that they're werewolves. Others know that something's wrong with them but think that they just have a bad alcohol addiction, which would explain all the blacking out and the weird injuries they get on every full moon.

- Their mortal weakness is silver—silver stakes, silver bullets, silver knives, silver letter openers, whatever, as long as it's silver. It's helpful if you can jam the silver straight into their heart, but you can get creative with that part. Decapitation with a silver axe, maybe.

- They have super strength, which is a given for pretty much any monster.

- They can jump upwards of fifteen feet, at least according to my buddy Peter who took down a pack of them in Denver. Then again, Peter did a lot of drugs back in the sixties, so as far as he knows a lot of things can jump upwards of fifteen feet.

• Their vision, hearing, and sense of smell are incredibly acute. Human blood especially pulls their triggers. They're a lot like vampires in that way, except that they're not photosensitive—a werewolf isn't afraid of light, they just happen to be afflicted only during the nighttime hours of a full moon, so sunlight's a nonissue for them.

• They transfer their infection through bites—if you're bitten by a werewolf, it's already too late. You're gonna become one too. Samuel Campbell had an old recipe for curing a human of vampirism, maybe there's something similar out there for werewolves . . . but if there is a real cure, I haven't heard of it. A few years back, Sam and Dean were protecting a girl named Madison from a werewolf, only to realize that Madison had already been turned. According to the lore they'd heard, killing the wolf that sired her would cure her, so they did just that. No dice. Even after they offed the thing, Madison still wolfed out, and Sam had to put her down.

• A werewolf's human host is otherwise unaffected by its affliction. Whereas a vampire is a vampire all the time, a werewolf can live a largely normal human life, as long as they lock themselves up before they change each full moon.

- They grow real fur, but it's not actual wolf fur. When Sam and Dean were investigating a potential werewolf case in Canonsburg, Pennsylvania, they found real wolf hair at the scene of a murder. While a lot of hunters mighta taken that as conclusive proof, the Winchester boys knew that werewolves are a hybrid creature –the fur they grow isn't real wolf hair.

At the time, there was nothing in the evidence that led me to believe it *wasn't* a werewolf, but I was still a baby hunter. I'd been involved in two supernatural incidents, both of them had ended with most everyone dead but me. This time, I had to do better. I wasn't going to let my assumptions drive my decision-making.

While I was at the scene, an agent from the Criminal Investigation Bureau (Japan's equivalent of the FBI) showed up and took over. They had reason to believe that a mental patient from a nearby lockup had escaped and was responsible for the killings. The guy commanded a lot of respect from the beat cops who had been running the show, but there was something off about him. His hair had a little too much gel, he was a little too young, he wore sneakers with his black suit and tie.

Whereas my pretext held up because I was an American claiming to be an American, I could tell this guy was a kid playing government agent. When he left the scene twenty minutes later, I was waiting for him at his car.

"You're here about the werewolf?" I asked him, point-blank.

I knew the guy spoke English (he had greeted me with the fluency of a native speaker earlier), but now he feigned ignorance.

"What is where? A wolf?" he said, or something like that. Don't quote me on any of this, most of my memories are Cheez Whiz recipes at this point.

He got in his car, tried to drive away, but I was in the passenger seat before he hit the gas. Asked him again. Told him I knew that it wasn't an escaped mental patient that was killing the girls.

The look he gave me, it was a mixture of annoyance and recognition. Like I was a brother-in-arms, but an annoying brother who he wished wouldn't drop in all the time. Nevertheless, he drove me back to his house, which was deep in the woods outside Tokyo. There, a dozen more hunters were waiting. They had quite the setup. It was like a Fortress of Hunter Solitude, with all manner of training equipment, lore books, even some computer equipment (which was in those days very primitive, but they had the bleeding edge stuff). I was the only outsider they'd ever let into their inner sanctum, and it showed on the faces of every man and woman there.

Why'd they bring me in? Because my reluctant driver thought that I had more information about what we were both hunting than I actually did. Once we got talking, he immediately regretted showing me the location of their base. For all he knew, *I* could be the creature that was killing those girls, and he just led me right to the home of the only people who could stop me. I made my case pretty effectively, explaining everything I'd been through. They had suspected that *Nishigo Maru* had been a victim of some kind of sea creature attack, and were all very interested in hearing the (long) story. When I finished, the oldest man there gave me a long, withering look, then took me into the next room.

Inside the chamber, there was a samurai sword. He explained (in Japanese, which by then I thankfully understood) that their brotherhood (and sisterhood) had been keeping the Japanese islands safe for many generations, and that this sword had been used to slay a great beast by his great-great-great-great-great-great-grandfather (probably there were even more greats in there than that). Ever since then, their family kept the secret of the supernatural—that all of the creatures in folklore were real—to themselves. They protected civilians while taking on incredible risks, and he respected me for trying to do the same. He put a lot of emphasis on the word "trying," which I didn't exactly appreciate, but whatever.

They called themselves "ハンター," or *hantaa*, which means hunter. Not that original, but what are you gonna do? Looking back, the lore he told me about the "great beast" his ancestor had slain with that samurai sword makes me think it mighta been a *dragon*, which made that blade a *dragon sword*. If current events are any indication, you'll need to brush up on dragon history . . . I'll get to writing some down as soon as I can.

We ate a meal together, and my Japanese brethren told me that I was wrong about the werewolf—it was actually an *okami* we were hunting. They're a cousin of the werewolf, but specific to Japan. Most of their MO is similar, but the method of dispatching them is very different. Made me real glad that I didn't try to go after the thing myself, or things woulda gone pear-shaped right quick.

To kill an okami, you need a bamboo dagger, blessed by a Shinto priest. In Japan, those aren't hard to find. In fact, one of the hunters at the table was himself a Shinto priest. In America and other parts, good friggin' luck. Probably could get one imported, but if I learned anything on board *Nishigo Maru*, it was that the boat trip between San Fran and Tokyo is looooong.

Once you've got your bamboo dagger and had it blessed, you need to stab the okami seven times. Not six. Not eight. *Seven*. Why? I don't know. The folks at the Japanese Ninja Hunter Lodge didn't know, either, they just told me over and over to stab the okami seven times, so I took notice.

I thanked the hantaa for their hospitality and asked what they planned to do next. Go after the thing? Collect more evidence? I was new to the game, so I wasn't sure what a proper hunter would do. Their answer? They weren't gonna do squat. I was.

See, the old man told me that I had a dark spot

on my soul, or something to that effect. That I wasn't going to be able to start moving on from Karen's death until I'd been able to take retribution on some of the dark forces in the world. Mostly, I think, he knew I was a crappy hunter and I needed to get better quick or die trying.

So out I went, into the wilds, armed with a bamboo dagger and a prayer. I spent the next week chasing leads, going from one clue to the next as quickly as I could. Eventually, another victim was found. I felt terrible, seeing as the hantaa clan had trusted me to find the okami and put it down before anyone else got hurt.

I redoubled my efforts, and was able to find a solid lead—all the women had gone to the same bar within twenty-four hours of being killed. The okami musta been following women home from the bar and attacking them when they were alone.

A flannel-wearing white dude at a hip Japanese bar attracts a lot of attention, let me tell you what. Usually, that'd be a bad thing. In this case, I used the attention to talk to as many people as possible about the bar's regulars, ask if any of them had been acting strangely recently. The bartender pointed me in the direction of a particularly shy-looking man of about twenty-three. He sat in the corner and nursed a beer, eying women as they walked by.

Just before closing time, the guy up and left. I followed him out to the alley, where he lit up a cigarette and waited in the shadows. It's hard to follow someone discreetly when they're already in the best hiding spot, but I made do. Sure enough, after a few minutes of waiting, he started to tail a woman as she walked home.

I tailed them both, interrupted his stalking just as he closed in on her. Right as I was pulling the bamboo dagger from my jacket, he screamed out something I wasn't expecting: "Surprise!"

From out of nowhere, there were suddenly twenty-five people all around me. They were all holding noise makers and balloons, one of 'em had a friggin' *cake*. Weirdest surprise birthday party I've ever seen, but hey, that's Japan.

I started to walk back to the bar, feeling like a damn fool, when the bat hit the back of my head.

· · · · ·

Thanks a lot, Americans, for introducing baseball to Japan. Now they can't get enough of the sport, and that meant that the baseball bat that the okami used to clock my noggin was of very high quality. The better to give me a concussion with.

I could only have been out for a minute, because when I came to, the okami was still trying to drag me to a secluded area. Guess he didn't want to rip me to shreds where the birthday partygoers could see. He was about thirty years old, and a salaryman. His suit was nice, like he made a decent living, and his hair was impeccably styled. All this murdering must have been his side job.

So there's a lesson for you—first of all, you can't tell the monster just from his appearance. Shady looking guys could be legit, businessmen can be monsters. Second, standing out like a sore thumb while you're hunting can just as easily lead the monster to you as it can lead you to the monster.

In this case, luck was on my side. This guy knew I was onto him, but he probably thought I was a cop. Had no idea how prepared I was for this encounter. A lot of monsters are completely unaware that there's even such a thing as hunters, since it's not like there's some orientation session they all have to go to when they find out they're monsters (. . . that we know of). The okami hadn't noticed that I'd come to, and was very surprised when I hooked my leg behind his foot, tripping him. I was on top of him in a second, reaching for my bamboo dagger—but it wasn't there. Balls. Musta dropped it when I got hit. I leaped off him, ran back towards the lighted area where he'd jumped me. A flying baseball bat hit me in the back of the knees, knocked me flat on my face.

But I'd been knocked down before, and this time I was determined to come out on top. I picked up the bat, hurled it back at the okami, who took it right in the face. No matter how big you are or how invulnerable to conventional weapons, that's gotta hurt.

Grabbing the bamboo dagger, I raced back to him, grappled with the beast as he bared his fangs. They were razor sharp and headed right for my carotid artery. I got the bamboo dagger between us and pushed it towards him as hard as I could, inch by inch, as he tried to reverse it and impale me instead.

I won. The dagger slipped out of his hands and I drove it right into his chest. He gasped in pain, and I pulled the dagger free and stabbed him again. And again, and a few more times, and . . . dammit. In my excitement, I'd forgotten how many times I stabbed him. Five? Six?

I was pretty sure it was six, so I gave him one, final, violent stab. His blood spurted out a hole in his back, I stabbed him so hard. Funny how quickly something like that becomes an accomplishment, and not evidence of being a sociopath.

The okami fell to the ground, dead. I waited a minute, catching my breath. In the distance, I could hear the party-group moving off into the night. I thought about how close I'd come to accidentally murdering that kid, and it gave me pause. Hunting is full of gray areas, and that's a big one. Sometimes, you're just not sure you've got the right guy. Even after you've put 'em in the ground, it can be a question mark. This time, I'd seen the fangs. I knew for sure, and it felt damn good. My first real victory.

. . . . .

Even in Japan, cell phones were an extreme rarity back then, so I was gonna have to handle the body all by myself. After retrieving a shovel I'd left near the bar, I found as secluded a spot as I could and started to dig. Two feet into the grave, I felt an itch on my leg, reached down to scratch it, and—the okami's fangs were in my leg. The bastard wasn't dead—I musta miscounted the stabs. I kicked him square in the jaw and had my bamboo dagger out in a heartbeat, buried it as deep in his sternum as I could. I'll skip to the end—this time, the critter was well and truly dead.

. . . . .

The hantaa were much more welcoming to me after I'd killed the okami, though "welcoming" for them don't mean the same thing as it does in my neck of the woods. They took me in to fully train me in their ways, but it felt more like boot camp than a bed and breakfast. I learned so much crap from them that I use every day it's not even funny. They were all about honor, which goes back to what I was saying before, about knowing you've got the right guy. "The right thing, the honorable thing," that's what the old man was always tellin' me.

We went on hunts together for a few months, most of the time with one of the hantaa taking the lead. I was happy to stand back and watch them work, see what details they noticed, what they didn't. A few times, I found things that they didn't. Those were the best days—when I felt like I could actually contribute something to a group that'd been doing this since friggin' Christopher Columbus was sailing the ocean blue.

To say that living in Japan was therapeutic is an understatement. So much of my life had been messed up by losing Karen, but being in a new place, an outsider in a strange land . . . it was like I'd started over. A whole new chance at life, but this time, I don't know, I felt like what I was doing mattered. I was changing the world for the better, one hunt at a time. 'Course, before Karen died I didn't know any of these problems even existed, but just because you don't know about something don't mean it won't kill you.

While I was there, we took down that okami, a *yama-otoko*, which is sort of like a cyclops and a troll mixed together, a *hinoenma*, which in America we call a succubus, and more than a few ghosts and vengeful spirits. Poltergeists are big in Japan, and if I had to guess why, I'd say it's because their culture can be so rigid. People there are polite, there's a strict social hierarchy, and people rarely deviate from it. If someone walks into a room, you formally greet them. Every time. It can wear on you a little bit, but I gotta say, it's a nice change from the way Americans can act sometimes. Like Romans under Romulus Augustus. Anyway, if you've lived your life constrained like that, it's no wonder some of them go a little bonkers in the afterlife, start stirring the pot in a way they never could when they were alive.

I loved living in Japan, but all good things must come to an end. There came a day when I'd learned about everything I could from the hantaa, and I booked my trip back to America. On a *plane*, if you're wondering. No way was I getting on another freighter.

RUFUS

WHEN I GOT BACK TO SIOUX FALLS, I spent a week just cleaning up the place. The house had been trashed before I left, and then I was gone for nearly a year, which didn't help. The dust alone was enough to make the place feel like a tomb. Which, in a way, it was.

My next order of business was to find Rufus Turner. He'd given me his contact info, but I'd smartly dropped it into the middle of the Pacific Ocean, so I had to use more unorthodox methods to find him. He's not the type of guy that's in the public phone book, and this was before you could do a person search on the Internet and have an answer in five seconds.

I used the same method I'd come up with in Japan—I gave him a reason to come to me. I started feeding stories to newspapers in the Sioux Falls area about cattle mutilations, trees being knocked over by dry lightning, huge black smoke clouds circling above farmland, the works. Every omen of demonic possession I could think of. Then, I waited.

It took Rufus three days to get to my place, and

boy was he surprised when I was waiting for him on the front porch. This is an understatement, but the man was not happy to see me. He'd let me in on a secret world that very few people ever get to hear anything about, only to have me run off without so much as a goodbye. He tried to track me down, but assumed I'd gotten myself killed, either by a monster or by drinking myself to death.

That said, convincing him to take me under his wing wasn't all that difficult. He still wanted a partner, and I'd learned quite a bit about hunting in my time abroad. As crazy as it seemed, there were things I could teach *him*. Not that he'd ever admit that.

He asked me a few questions before we set out on the road:

- "Are you willing to die for this?" I answered that it was the only thing I was willing to live for, which was good enough for him.

- "Are you willing to kill me, if I ask you to?" I told him about all the death I'd seen on *Nishigo Maru*, about the okami, about all the other things I'd seen. I understood what it meant to become a monster, and all the reasons it'd be better to die than be turned.

- "Do you like disco?" I guessed that he was hoping for a yes, so that's what I said. He told me to pack up my crap.

From that moment on, we were a team. Just like Sam and Dean, we rode around the country, helping people, hunting things while trying to get whatever enjoyment out of life that we could. That meant a lot of great times, but also a lot of terrible ones. Probably more terrible than great, but I knew that going in. It was a perfect partnership, until I screwed it all up. But I'll get to that.

SOMETHING GOOD

WHAT ELSE AM I FORGETTING to write down? I'll get back to Rufus in a minute, but my brain can only take so much reminiscing at once. Probably because so many of my memories are tragedies.

Maybe I should write down a good one. Something great that happened to me. The day I brought home Rumsfeld? He was my dog, a great mutt if you ever saw one, and friendly as all get-out, as long as you were coming in peace. He had a way of knowing when people were coming to make trouble, and that made him an even better dog.

I got him when he was just a pup, from a guy on I-29 coming north from Kansas City. He had pulled over to the side of the interstate, steam billowing from his engine compartment, and he flagged me down. Knowing a bit about cars as I did, I offered to help him fix his problem (broken serpentine belt, I had a spare in the truck that just happened to fit) and in exchange, he gave me one of the two pups he had kenneled in his backseat. I took Rumsfeld home, and . . .

Naw. That story ends in tragedy, too. Sam and Dean came by my place, looking for help with a little demon problem they had. Then the demon herself shows up at my door, Rumsfeld barks at her, then disappears. Never saw him again. Meg Masters, that was the demon. Haven't had another dog since, because no dog could live up to him. Except maybe Rumsfeld's brother, who's probably still out there somewhere.

Okay, so, something else then. Something useful. Shifters?

Here's some shifter lore:

- Every culture in the world has legends about shape-shifters. They call 'em different names, but they're all talking about the same beast. A man or woman who can take on the appearance of someone else, including their voice and mannerisms. They're one of the few monsters that are truly worldwide, like ghosts, and like vampires used to be before they were nearly hunted to extinction.

- Shifters have limits. They have to get close to the person they're going to mimic, or at least have access to a lot of imagery. When they change form, they shed their skin, hair, nails; everything on the outside must go. It's one of the more disgusting things you'll ever see, but not nearly as bad as knowing that someone is out there doing horrible things while wearing your face.

- They can only be killed by silver. A silver bullet or silver dagger to the heart are the best methods, but feel free to experiment if you ever get one tied up. The more ways to off them the better.

- Shifters can be identified by a flare in their eyes that appears on film or video. In a pinch, you can use the camera viewfinder on your cell phone to scan a crowd for them. This goes for a lot of other supernatural critters, as well—something about having their image captured reveals their true appearance.

- Some shifters are more adept and can shift faster and with less shedding than others. The alpha shape-shifter that Sam and Dean encountered was able to shift his appearance nearly instantaneously without shedding at all. The implication to me is that a shifter gets more talented as they get older. Practice makes perfect.

- They can hold a psychic connection with the person they're mimicking, as long as that person is still alive. The good news is that means they're less likely to kill you if they're taking on your appearance. The bad news is that they're using that psychic connection to know everything that you know, giving them the ability to walk right into your house and interact with your family in a way that is totally convincing. Every secret you have will be laid bare to the shifter.

That brings me to the case of the Douglas twins, from St. Cloud, Minnesota. Rufus and I were called in by a friend of his who saw an odd photo in a family album. The picture was of twin boys who were indistinguishable from each other, except for the odd eyes that one of 'em had in the photo. Rufus's friend, who he'd saved from a wendigo several years prior, knew enough about the "real" world to know that the odd appearance of the boy's eyes wasn't just red eye. The boy was a shifter.

When we got to the address where the twins lived, Rufus and I were confused. It was a gated retirement community. Enthusiastic old fellas were hauling out their golf clubs to play eighteen holes when we came through the door and they pointed us in the direction of the Douglas twins' rooms. When we found them, they were in the middle of a heated game of bingo. Not knowing what else to do, Rufus and I waited for the game to end before cornering them. This is the photo Rufus was sent: ⟶

The Douglas twins were now eighty-one years old. That picture was taken God knows how long ago, and there'd been no reports of strange disappearances or unexplained murders around where the

brothers had lived their entire lives. One of the twins was a shifter, but as far as we could tell, he'd never hurt a soul.

I bet you're expecting this story to take a crazy turn, but you're wrong. After questioning them for a few hours, spending a day at the city records office and the library looking through old newspapers, we didn't have any evidence that Charles Douglas, the shifter, had ever done anything wrong.

He'd been raised by humans, and turned out alright. When we asked the brothers flat-out, they admitted that he was different from most folks, but that he'd never used his abilities to harm anyone. He was a good monster.

We let him live. He was eighty-one, what was the worst that could happen?

You know what? That actually was a good memory.

THE RULES

RIDING WITH RUFUS IN THE EIGHTIES, I learned one thing—the man liked rules. He had a set of them for every occasion, and a day didn't go by without me breaking one and getting a lecture about it. It got especially annoying a few years in, when I wasn't just an apprentice anymore—I was more than capable of handling a hunt by myself, but still, without fail, the lectures . . .

RULE #1: IT IS WHAT IT LOOKS LIKE.

When we first started riding together, there were still a few vampire nests around the country. By the time we went our separate ways, they were thought to be extinct. But in between there was a gray period, when other hunters were constantly claiming to have killed the very last vamp on earth.

Outside of Salt Lake City, we were following up on reports of several teens being killed, their throats ripped to shreds, most of their blood drained. My first instinct was wendigo, even though the bloodletting wasn't usually their bag. There were some other clues that pointed towards a Native American connection, but my head's getting a little fuzzy on that part. All you need to know is that conventional wisdom at the time said that vampires had died out, but Rufus refused to believe it. "It is what it looks like," he said. Always was, always will be. The simplest answer is the most likely one, and in that particular case, that meant vamp.

Vampires have been part of human mythology for thousands of years—they're one of those elemental evil forces that we've feared since we knew how to be afraid.

However, most of that lore is wrong.

- Vamps aren't afraid of crosses. That's demons. Same with the Lord's name.

- Scratch garlic off your list, too.

- They have reflections, just like everybody else.

- They don't have two tiny little namby-pamby teeth on top to bite with. They have shark teeth. Really, really nasty and sharp shark teeth that can tear your throat out just as easily as you chew a grape. They retract, so as not to draw attention when the vampire is trying to be incognito.

- They won't burn up in the sun, but it does hurt them. It's more like a bad sunburn than anything. That means they're active at night, unless they're being really bold. If you do hear of a vampire hunting during the day, it may be one of their cousins instead.

- They don't need to be welcomed into your house to come in. They'll just break down the door. What kind of overly polite monsters did people think they were?

- They can't be killed with a stake to the heart. This is the biggie. Everybody and their uncle carries around wooden stakes to take down vamps, but it won't even hurt 'em. You've got to . . .

- Decapitate them. It's the only way to kill a vampire. Take their head clean off. Now, the way you go about that is up to you, and I encourage you to be creative, as always.

- They do need human blood to live. Meaning they often have to move from town to town to avoid detection and keep up their blood supply, often—

- Traveling in packs. One human can feed several

SUPERNATURAL

vamps, and they wouldn't want to waste their precious food supply, so they work together. They're one of the more communal monsters in the menagerie, and seem to have a strong social bond between members of the pack. They're even said to mate for life, which, when you're more or less immortal, is quite a commitment.

- They aren't always all bad. Sam and Dean ran into a vamp named Lenore who was able to control her blood lust, and she fed off cattle instead.

- They're vulnerable to "dead man's blood," which is exactly what it sounds like. Since fresh human blood is what gives them life (or whatever you wanna call their undead state), the blood from a dead human nullifies that effect, causing them to be weakened and slowed, but it won't kill them.

- Vampires are turned, not born. As far as we know anyway, the only way to make a new vampire is by feeding a human a vampire's blood.

- Vampirism is curable. It's not pretty, but as long as the newly turned vamp hasn't had a sip of human blood yet, they can be turned back into a human. Samuel Campbell has the exact recipe, so I guess that means it's now in my library somewhere. What I know is that the cocktail requires the blood of the vamp who turned you, which might be harder to retrieve than it seems.

So, how did that case outside of Salt Lake City turn out? Rufus was right, and we were looking for a vamp—but only one. The rest of his nest had been wiped out by Daniel Elkins, a hunter who specialized in tracking and killing vampires. When we caught up with the remaining vamp, he practically begged us to off him—his vampire bride was one of the first to be killed by Elkins, and he couldn't bear going on without her. I knew the feeling, and obliged him. Seeing the smile on his face as his head was cut off . . . that was messed up.

RULE #2: KNOW THEM BETTER THAN THEY KNOW YOU.

I learned this gem in Topeka, Kansas, when we visited the Arthur Mansion, a notoriously haunted estate that had provided fodder for an entire generation of daring children. Each year, on the tenth of August, kids would dare each other to go inside the house and stay for an entire hour.

We jumped on the case when some of those kids came out of the place *covered in blood*. It wasn't their own, but it sure as hell was somebody's, and nobody had a rational explanation for it. The children claimed that a spirit had hovered over them and threatened to pull their souls straight out of their chests if they didn't leave the house. They did exactly what I woulda done—they ran. Right through what they described as a "tunnel of blood and guts." Sounded like a poltergeist to me.

The lore:

- Spirits and ghosts are the remnant of a human soul that hasn't crossed over to heaven or hell. They have unfinished business that they have to attend to before they can move on, and that traps them on earth.

- They're already dead, so don't bother trying to kill them.

- You can, however, make them cross over. Some ghosts are tied to this plane because some piece of them remains here—physical remains, some object that held special significance to them, anything that can be a symbol of that person.

- Salting and burning a person's remains will banish their spirit. Make sure you get *all* of them, though, or the spirit will remain. If the person was an organ donor, even their donated kidney can come back to (literally) haunt its new owner.

- Ghosts can't travel, except under special circumstances. Generally, they're tied to the place where they died or the place where their remains are located. Certain ghosts, however, have learned to "ride" humans away from the spot where they're trapped, letting them move around the outside world. In the case of the haunted kidney, wherever the kidney went, so too went the ghost.

- You can also help the spirit resolve whatever it is that's keeping them here. That's usually easier said than done, especially since it often involves vengeance on the person who killed them or a person who tormented them as a human.

- Ghosts can't cross a salt line.

- They can also be temporarily dissipated by blasting 'em with rock salt. Keep a few shells loaded at all times, you never know when you'll need them.

- EMF (electromagnetic field) meters can detect the presence of a ghost or spirit.

- Iron also keeps spirits at bay. An iron crowbar is a good thing to keep in your trunk for a couple reasons, but that tops the list. One swing with it will dissipate a ghost for a couple of minutes.

At the Arthur Mansion, we were dealing with a spirit more powerful than your garden-variety ghost, so we planned accordingly. We brought enough salt to kill a horse, our EMF meters, shotguns, iron bars, and all the local lore on the house. Once inside, we discovered things were more complicated than they seemed.

Forty years prior, there had been a mass suicide at the house. At least, that's what the papers claimed. As we searched the house, we found evidence that the people had actually been *murdered*. In one room, scratch marks covered the door—scratch marks from human fingernails. Someone had carved the words "It's coming for us" into the wall. In another room, a pile of gnawed-on bones was hidden in an oak chest. Chewing on a bone was beyond the abilities of a spirit or poltergeist, so what were we facing? Let's skip ahead a second to—

RULE #3: IT CAN BE BOTH.

As in, if something leaves all the telltale signs of a werewolf, but one of the victims has a hole from a wraith spike on her forehead, maybe you're dealing with both. I know, crazy to think, but there are towns that have multiple infestations at once. You could be hunting a wendigo while a rougarou's setting up his campsite right next to you.

In this case, we were dealing with something *really* strange. We pieced together what had happened forty years ago—a monster of unknown origin had trapped a group of friends in the house during a dinner party. It killed them, one by one, making each death look like a suicide. When the local media got word, there was a frenzy. People from all over the country came to the house to look through the windows (the house itself had been boarded up after the police ruled the deaths suicides), and that led a man by the name of Gareth McIntosh to the mansion. Gareth wasn't just any tourist, he was a hunter. He felt that the events at the Arthur Mansion were highly suspicious, and he broke in to investigate. What happened next is a mystery, but the end result is clear—Gareth failed.

He was killed by whatever monster haunted the halls, but his unfinished business, finding and killing the creature, forced his spirit to remain in the house. Now, the monster and Gareth's ghost were locked in a decades-long battle for control of the mansion, and we'd just stepped into the middle of it.

That brings us back around to Rule #2: Know them better than they know you. You always want to know more about the monster you're hunting than they know about you, or they have the advantage. In this case, we were playing catch-up as we searched the house, while Gareth knew every one of our tricks. He was, after all, a hunter himself. If he didn't want us there, he would be able to counter any move we used against him.

It started with our EMF meters. They started acting wonky as soon as we walked in the door, but the readings were guiding us in a very clear direction—the basement. If not for my paranoia, Gareth's plan would have worked. He'd used his own EMF signature to lead us right into a booby trap, a room with a door that only opened from the outside. I caught the door as it swung shut, barely saving us from a few very unpleasant days together ending in some awkward conversations about whether we were allowed to eat each other once the other died.

Next, he burst the pipes in the bathroom as we were searching it, soaking us and our salt supplies. Since salt dissolves so easily in water, all of our reserves washed down the drain.

It was like that for three hours—a cat and mouse

game that ended with Rufus and me in the attic, facing a very old and very cranky monster that I swear was a Minotaur. Rufus says it was just a funky-looking wendigo, but I know what I saw. The thing came at us, but it moved slowly. We were able to outrun it, finding our way to a bedroom on the upper level. Inside of it, we found Gareth's skeleton. What was left of it, anyway. If only we still had our salt, we could have salted and burned his remains then and there. Life's like that, I guess.

Instead, Rufus had a brilliant idea. We didn't need to get rid of the ghost, we needed to kill the Minotaur (or wendigo, or whatever). If we did that, Gareth's unfinished business would be resolved, and we could go on our way. The only problem was killing something that we couldn't really identify.

That's where *my* brilliant idea came into play. We knew someone with decades of hunting expertise under his belt, and he was right here in the house. If we could just *ask* him, maybe he could tell us how to kill the creature. After all, he must have spent the last forty years thinking about it. As a poltergeist, he could only do so much to manipulate the world around him; clearly he wasn't able to do whatever was required to take out the monster.

Cut to—a séance. We were taking an awful risk, since summoning Gareth's spirit could just make him angrier, but it was the only way. Rufus led the ceremony, while I kept an iron crowbar in hand, ready to start swinging if things went south.

As Rufus droned on in Latin, the room got colder. A spirit was coming. When Gareth appeared, it was in his human form. He didn't seem nearly as intimidating that way. Make no mistake, though, any spirit who's been trapped in an incorporeal state that long by himself is going to be more than a little nuts. Gareth was no exception. When he spoke, it was like hearing a throaty growl mixed with his words. He gave us the usual ghost spiel, "Get out of the house," "This place will be your tomb," "You have stepped on unholy ground," blah blah blah. Things got interesting when I asked him about the critter in the attic. He hissed at me, like he was a cat thrown in a bathtub, but pulled himself together. Said that the thing was his alone to kill.

That was no help, I thought, and got ready to swing the iron bar through Gareth and end our fiesta. Rufus spoke up. Asked if we could at least *help* Gareth fight the creature. To my great surprise, Gareth nodded. Said there was something we could do.

There are Latin incantations that can break a demon's bond to its host body. In the same way, there was an incantation that could *forge* a bond between a spirit and a host, allowing the spirit to ride a human like a surfboard, controlling their actions and seeing through the human's eyes. If we would do that for Gareth, he could fight and kill the creature, and then his spirit would be free to pass on to the other side.

Rufus was all for it, said he'd volunteer to be the host. I warned him that there were several pretty gaping holes in the logic. First off, what's to keep Gareth from *holding on* to Rufus's body after he's done? Also, the last time Gareth tried to kill that creature, it *murdered him to death*. His track record was not great.

But Rufus was a better talker than listener. He agreed, and we did the Latin ritual, and suddenly my friend Rufus was talking with an Irish accent and really enjoying his newfound ability to breathe air.

I'd love to tell you exactly how the rest of the hunt went, but I spent the whole time locked in a broom closet. Gareth spent forty years wanting to avenge his own murder, he wasn't taking any chance that I'd kill the thing for him.

When he finally let me out, Rufus's accent had returned to normal, and he told me that the beast was dead. Gareth's unfinished business was complete, so he'd passed on to the other side of the veil.

For a solid month, I was sure he was faking it, and that Gareth was still in there somewhere. I even tried tempting him with Guinness and bangers 'n mash, until Rufus got annoyed and made me stop. It was for his own good.

RULE #4: NEVER HIT THE SAME TOWN TWICE.

This one's simple. We followed a succubus to Lincoln, Nebraska, and ended up getting chased out of town by a cadre of furious husbands—a year prior, Rufus had been in Lincoln cleaning up a coven of witches when a spell went haywire. He was supposed to be making a hex bag to shield him from the magic of the coven, but instead made a hex bag that caused every nearby woman to fall deeply in love with him. Rufus being Rufus, he didn't notice for a few days, and assumed that the women of Lincoln were simply more open with their sexuality than in other cities. Rufus's girlfriend had broken up with him for the tenth time earlier that month, and he did a lot of rebounding. The man got more action in a week than he had in his entire life, and didn't for a second think that something unnatural was afoot.

It wasn't until two furious husbands knocked on his motel door that Rufus realized he had a problem. He was out of town within fifteen minutes and vowed never to return. That is, until our case took us there. It's really hard to work a case when you have guys following you around with brass knuckles. We ended up having to call Martin Creaser to go after the succubus instead—and Rufus never went back to Lincoln.

RULE #5: IT AIN'T DEAD TILL IT'S IN FIVE PIECES.

Speaking of witches, St. Louis is crawling with them. I don't know why, but it's true. You can't go a block in that town without tripping over a hex bag. Rufus and I hunted one there who was exceptionally nasty—she'd been using spells to turn all the food in her neighbors' houses to acid. I don't know what her motivation was—that had to be hurting her home value.

When we finally tracked her down, I put a bullet

in her head. You'd think that'd be enough, but nooooo. The bitch stood back up, telekinetically pinned me to the wall and started twisting around my insides.

The good thing about witches is that they're usually easy to kill. See, witches aren't monsters, they're just folks. Folks who, for whatever reason, are total jackasses and use black magic to further their own ends while screwing over and killing people who they don't like.

That's why we burn them. They have it coming. It's not that a bullet won't kill them, it's that burning them hurts more. Back in the day, people had all kinds of crazy theories about witches—that they'd float if you tried to drown them, that they could control people's minds, that they rode around on broomsticks. None of that's true.

In the case of the St. Louis witch, she musta been way higher up the food chain than we thought. Once they develop telekinesis, you know a witch or warlock isn't screwing around. Luckily, being a witch doesn't give them extra brains. Rufus had snuck in the back door and chopped the lady's head off with an axe. Then he chopped her in half. Then he chopped her a few more times.

"It ain't dead till it's in five pieces," he said. I loved Rufus.

WHERE AM I NOW?

JUST HAD A FLASH OF SOMETHING. The woman's face, the water woman from the swamp. She was holding out her hand, and . . . I don't know, it felt like I was getting pulled apart.

I have a confession to make. I don't even remember starting to write this book. A few hours ago, I had to re-read the whole thing just to know what I was doing and what I'd already said.

For a few minutes, I actually thought about going to the hospital. As if they'd be able to do anything. This is . . . unsettling for me. I'm not one to ask people for help, but right about now, all I wish is that I had someone I could talk to.

Maybe I should drive back to Ashland. A part of me is afraid I wouldn't even make it there. If I *did* get there, I wouldn't know what to look for. Why are some things so clear, and others so muddy?

I have to keep going. Keep writing. Something will make it all fit together.

JOHN WINCHESTER

IT WAS DURING MY TIME RIDING with Rufus that I first met a hunter by the name of John Winchester. He had been steadily building a reputation for the few years he was active (1983 on), and so I was curious to see what kind of man he was. The answer? Complicated. At the time, I had no idea he had kids. Just that he'd taken on a fool's quest to hunt a yellow-eyed demon.

We joined up with him on a hunt in Oregon, in an unincorporated area outside of Baker City. A construction crew had gone missing while trying to tear down an abandoned house. The previous owners had also gone missing, so we smelled something supernatural in the air.

John struck me as a levelheaded sort of guy, but he was so driven that it was hard to keep up with him. He was inside the house before we'd even opened our trunk, and he was running out cursing before I chambered a round.

The house was, to skip to the crazy, *alive*. At some point in its history, it'd been imbued with consciousness and a self-preservation instinct, and was simply not going to allow itself to be torn down.

We tried every damn thing we could think of to bring it to the ground. Fire, axes, and sledgehammers; John even threw a grenade or two inside, but each time, the house would react, find some way to protect itself.

I got a chance to talk to John as we took a lunch break. As soon as we were "off the clock," out came the pictures of his boys, Dean and Sam. He was so proud of them, Dean for following so closely in his footsteps, Sam for being so good at school, despite moving around so much. He missed them. Hadn't seen them in a week and a half, had left them with a housekeeper at a hotel in Housatonic, Massachusetts.

That was my first taste of the side of John that I couldn't stand. I empathized with him, and understood the need to get vengeance for his dead wife, but he had kids to look after. He shouldn't have left them to be raised by strangers. I told him as much, and he stood up and walked away.

Finally, somebody had an idea, can't remember who. Termites. Lots and lots of termites. Let them loose inside, where they could slowly eat the house's skeleton away. It was brought up that the termite plan was a cop-out, that it could take years to work, and that it very well could fail just like the hand grenades, but none of us wanted to get bitten in half by a garage door, so there we were.

I went by that house a few years back, it was just a pile of rotted lumber. Sometimes the cop-out is the best way out.

THE SHIT LIST

SPEAKING OF JOHN, here's something important I definitely don't want to forget—all the people I can't friggin' stand. I've been around the sun a few times, made my share of friends and way more than my share of enemies, and these are the ones who'll probably dance on my grave when I'm gone. Listen up, ya idjits, I'd do the same to you. (I'm not including people that're already dead. What would be the use?)

Kurt Dremler. For leaving me alone to fight that *shtriga* in Orlando, the cowardly bastard.

Jason Larson. That prick has owed me more money than anyone else I've ever known, but in tiny increments spread out over fifteen years. Every time I see him, the guy needs five bucks for something. We go to lunch, he forgot his wallet. I meet him to go fishing, he forgot his tackle, needs to stop at the bait shop to buy more. He pays it back . . . eventually, after great prodding.

Alexis Sinclair. The woman that owns the land directly behind mine. This woman has caused more problems for me than most monsters. She just won't listen to reason. It's gonna make noise, lady, it's a car crusher! Geez. Call the county zoning board one more time, why don'tcha?

Derek Knightley. For that time with the rawhead. He owes me a new shotgun, a new set of tail lights, and some of my dignity back.

Michael Wal. He knows why.

Sheriff Mills. How many times do I have to explain to her—I drive that way on purpose. It's gotten so bad that they pull me over now just for coming into town. And I may have been in a few bar fights and drank a little too much a few times over the last *twenty years*, but that's not bad if you average it out. Like I always tell her, if I'm gonna get *really* drunk, I'm gonna do it in the comfort of my own home. Mills has redeemed herself a bit in the last few years, but I'd still love to give her a piece of my mind. Too bad I don't have any of those pieces left.

M. Night Shyamalan. Guy owes me $8.50 for *Lady in the Water*.

TASTES LIKE CHICKEN

MAN, MY MEMORY IS REALLY GOING. I'm just seeing flashes now, some things I understand, some things I don't. I just had this vision of Rufus wrestling with a Komodo dragon . . . when did that happen?

Wait.

Right. Eighties. I remember it now. This is actually a good one, I should write it down before I forget.

See, sometimes, this job is gross. Sometimes it's *really* gross. And sometimes, you're hunting a *nagual*.

Naguals are a Mesoamerican cryptid that have been known to migrate as far north as Kansas and Colorado, if the weather is right. They prefer hot and muggy, and unlike a lot of critters, they operate both in daytime and at night. Their trick is to blend in with humans most of the time, when they're not in their animal forms. They're distant cousins of the shifter, werewolf, and skinwalker—all of them have the ability to change their shapes, but the nagual are more varied than skinwalkers and werewolves . . . they can transform into a buncha different animals.

Depends on the personality of the nagual, I guess, but I've heard of one changing into a snake, one into a bird, one into a dog (though that coulda just been a misidentified skinwalker).

Naguals have a slightly different MO from skinwalkers—they will kill humans, but prefer to feed in whatever their native animal form is. If they're a snake, they eat mice, if they're a bird, they eat worms. You get the idea. Nagual are dangerous not because of their feeding habits, but because of their method of procreation.

A nagual and another nagual can meet, fall in love, want to have cute little blue-eyed babies together, and everything is sunshine and roses until they realize that the "birds and the bees" part doesn't work . . . because they're literally a bird and a bee. They can try to breed all they like, it ain't gonna happen. A female nagual could get pregnant in her human form, but as soon as she turns into her animal form, she'd miscarry—and their transformations aren't voluntary. Sooner or later, they'll lose the baby.

So, to keep their numbers up, they have to recruit. They're a lot like vamps in that respect. If they want a *baby* baby, they'll have to steal one from a human couple and turn it.

After several children disappeared in the Phoenix metro area, Rufus and I got on the case. A few factors led us to believe a nagual might be involved—the family of the first disappeared girl said that they'd found an iguana outside their house and brought it inside, and when their daughter was kidnapped, the kidnapper took the iguana too. Didn't seem like someone would bother taking the lizard if they were in the middle of a kidnapping, so we started to think that maybe the lizard *was* the kidnapper.

We hunted the thing across three counties before we heard a police radio squawk about a disabled vehicle on a desert road—the copper said that the vehicle was an old RV, empty except for a lizard, a couple cats, two ravens, a koala, and a marmoset. Sounded to me and Rufus like we were chasing a whole pack of naguals, and that they'd already turned the stolen kids.

Here's the most important part of the story: once you've been bitten by a nagual in their animal form, you become one of them within a day. There are ways to stop the transformation, but *only if you get to the victim before they change*. Since the kids were already changed, they were already monsters. There was nothing we could do for them except stop them from doing the same thing to someone else. Sounds harsh, I know, but there ain't another way around it. If I was forced to become an armadillo for half my life, I'd want it all to end pronto.

When we got to the RV, the lizard and the koala were valiantly attempting to use a jack and tire iron to replace their blown tire. Like I said, naguals can't change at will, so if they were stuck in their animal forms, that was that. We thought it was an open-and-shut case, we'd just gank the things and move on with our business, until things got weird.

Rufus had pulled his Desert Eagle on the koala, which was the strangest damn sight I ever did see, and I've seen some strange. As he was talking to the thing (telling it to step away from the tire iron, if I can remember correctly), I was searching the inside of the RV. The two ravens flew the coop, and I chased after them. I fired a few wild shots, mighta nicked one of 'em, but both got away. Then I heard Rufus yell out, "The damn thing bit me!"

I turned to the sound, saw him wrestling with this giant Komodo dragon—it musta been laying out on the cool asphalt under the RV. It'd taken a chunk out of Rufus's arm, and he was bleeding pretty bad. I took a few shots (using silver bullets—as cousins of weres and shifters, silver's the only thing that'll hurt 'em) and managed to put down the dragon. The rest of the animals went into a friggin' frenzy like I've never seen. Rufus and I both fired like crazy, took the whole pack down, minus those two ravens (one of which, I swear to God, came back and took a crap on me while I was shooting).

In all the chaos, I hadn't even noticed that the koala had scratched me. Those things look all cuddly and friendly, but they're little jags, every last one of 'em.

Rufus and I were both infected. We would both turn into naguals by the end of the day if we didn't do something about it ASAP. This is where the gross part comes in. . . .

The only cure for nagual venom is to consume the flesh of the nagual who bit you. For Rufus, that was the Komodo dragon. For me, it was the stupid koala. But here's the kicker—when they die, naguals transform halfway in between their two forms. Half man, half beast. Half yuppie tax attorney, half Komodo dragon. Half hippy chick, half koala.

We had to eat them.

Grossest meal of my life, and I already told you about the seaweed.

So if you find yourself in the same situation, make the most of it, like Rufus and I did. We got ourselves to a kitchen as soon as we could, cooked up as close to a gourmet meal as possible with the nagual as a base.

Here's the recipe:

ELEGANT CRITTER WITH MONSTER MASHED POTATOES

You gotta eat the whole monster. Sorry, there's no way around it. But the truth is, it really does taste like chicken, if you cook it just right. If you ever find yourself with time to spare and you don't have a critter on hand, just substitute chicken breasts and good old condensed cream of chicken soup and you'll have yourself a feast that would impress any lady. First meal I ever made Karen. If it was good enough for her, it's good enough for any of you.

Ingredients:
2 whole nagual breasts, skinned and boned
8 slices Swiss cheese
1 cup condensed cream of critter soup
*   (instructions below)*
1/4 cup dry white wine (or whiskey if
*   that's all you've got)*
2 cups seasoned breadcrumbs (I use
*   Wonder Bread)*
1/3 cup melted butter

1. *First step, kill the damn critter. If you got bit and it ran off, hurry and chase it down. Otherwise, go ahead and substitute in the chicken and say your prayers. It'd make a fine last meal for any man. Especially if you're about to turn into a koala and be stuck eating eucalyptus leaves for the rest of your life.*
2. *Once you've made sure the thing's dead, cut it up. Put the breasts aside. Place the rest in a big pot and cover with water. Let simmer for an hour, if you have time. If you're starting to feel the effects of the venom, you can get by with a half hour, but you'll lose some flavor.*
3. *To make the condensed soup base, strain the meat and bones and place 1 1/2 cups of critter broth in a medium-sized saucepan; bring to a boil. Add 1/2 cup of whole milk*

or cream, and season to taste. In a bowl, whisk together an additional cup of milk or cream and 3/4 of a cup of flour. Add to the boiling mixture and continue to whisk briskly until the mixture boils again and thickens.

4. Place the breasts in a 9x13 ceramic baking dish and top with cheese slices. Combine soup base and wine and pour over the cheese. Mix together the breadcrumbs and butter and sprinkle over the nagual, cheese, and sauce.

5. Bake at 350 degrees for one hour. While it bakes, prepare the potatoes and gravy.

MONSTER MASHED POTATOES

Cut and peel one-pound of Yukon gold potatoes. Add to a large pot of boiling water. Cook until soft, about thirty minutes. This is where things get messy. While the potatoes cook, use an immersion blender to combine the remaining pieces of the nagual. The bone should have softened enough so that the hardest part will be blending it without making yourself sick. It's just like making food for a baby. Grind it up and pretend it's applesauce. When it's as smooth as can be, turn the pot back on and bring to a simmer. It will be pretty thick, so thin it out to a palatable consistency. Normally, I like to add a can of cream of mushroom soup to my gravy, but if you don't have that lying around, milk will do. When the potatoes are done, mash them up and add as much butter and salt and garlic as you can. Take the nagual out of the oven, put it on top of the taters, smother it in gravy, and tell yourself it's chicken.

ALPHAS

MONSTERS AIN'T LIKE PEOPLE. Some of them try to blend, some of them succeed better than others, but one constant is this: they operate by different rules than us. They have their own social hierarchies and customs and wants, many of which we'll never understand. The biggest example of that are the alphas. For years and years, hunters assumed that each nest of vamps they killed was separate, a solitary kingdom that had no connection with the other nests around the world. That was before we found out that every single one of the creatures had a psychic connection to the boss vamp, the alpha.

Other creatures have the same system. Werewolves, skinwalkers, wendigos, shifters, ghouls, djinn, wraiths, they all have alphas.

How do you fight one? You don't. If you think killing a regular monster is hard, imagine fighting one that's been on earth for literally thousands upon thousands of years, honing their abilities and sharpening their claws/fangs/whatever.

In every encounter we've had with an alpha, we've been outclassed. If the Winchester boys can't take one down, I hate to break it to you, but you don't have a snowflake's chance in hell.

DRAGONS

THE STRANGEST THING ABOUT THIS . . . *sickness* I've got, or whatever you want to call it, is what I remember and what I don't. I remember the sandwich Rufus ate for breakfast the day after we took down Gareth McIntosh's ghost, but I can't recall my mother's face. Memory loss wouldn't be so bad if you could choose which things not to remember. I'd like to remember my mother, if only to have someone to blame for the way I turned out.

One woman you'll never forget once you meet her? Eleanor Visyak. Ellie is a professor of medieval studies at SFU, and an expert at so many things it makes my head hurt. Or maybe that's the whiskey. Or the memory loss. Anyway, if you need to know anything about dragons, she's the one you wanna ask. Why dragons? Because they're the flavor of the week. After hundreds of years, they're suddenly back on the scene, and we're not quite sure why.

A lot of hunters like to go it alone, figure things out for themselves. But that's where we get in trouble, why I'm writing all this junk down. There's too much out there that can take you by surprise. We need to get organized. There's dragons? Really? That's the sort of thing no hunter should turn around and find breathing down his neck.

Wouldn't it be great if somebody had friggin' *jotted something down* about half the creatures we come across? I can't exactly picture Dean writing in his diary every night (though I can picture him stealing Sam's and making fun of him for what he wrote). This isn't about writing down your feelings. But at least keep track of the important stuff. And the point is, it's all important. If you don't have time to write down everything you know about dragons, at least write down where you got your information. That's what I'm gonna do here. I don't know jack squat about dragons, but I know they're important. I know they're *gonna* mean something, so I'll point you in the right direction—Eleanor Visyak.

This is an excerpt from an unpublished manuscript she wrote called *Dragon Lore, Fact and Fiction*. It's not the version of dragons you'll read about in *The Hobbit*—it's the real deal, straight from the only person who still believed in them *before* they made their sudden reappearance. After she submitted her manuscript for publication, SFU asked her if she wanted to be transferred from Medieval Studies to the Creative Writing department. We'll see how they feel about it once they've been burned to a crisp by one touch from a dragon's hand. I hate to admit it, but even I wrote this off as bull when I first heard about it. It wasn't until recently that I went back and dusted off a copy of the text.

DRAGON LORE: FACT AND FICTION
Written by Professor Eleanor Visyak

Chapter 9: The Dragon Sword

No matter what Hollywood tells us, there is only one way to slay a dragon: with a sword forged from the blood of a dragon. Which raises the question, where did the first dragon sword come from?

In artistic representations throughout history and from around the world, dragons are shown as a conglomeration of human fears: the head of a snake, the body of a lion, the breath of the Devil. While lions and snakes are not relative to this anecdote, the story of the dragon sword does involve a conflict not unlike the infamous rebellion of Lucifer. Like the impetuous archangel, who found it disgraceful that God should so heavily favor humans over the other creatures of the earth, many dragons likewise believed it unfair that creatures as powerful and majestic as them be confined to the darkest and dankest parts of the planet. It was not a love of the dark that drove dragons into caves and dank places that humans rarely inhabited. In the beginning, things simply *were*. It wasn't until later that angels, humans, demons, and dragons began their existential explorations into *why* things were that way. Dragons could set an entire village to flame with a touch of a hand. Why must they live in the darkness? So they grew in strength and numbers and planned to move into the light.

One dragon, Hypolyes, saw the inherent order in the status quo. To each species, a space was apportioned, and the dragons were no more entitled to the entirety of Creation than the humans, angels, or demons. Hypolyes went to purgatory, where the Dragon Mother resided, and told her of the pernicious plans of the other dragons. The Mother realized that she had instilled too much power into her beloved dragons; if no one could kill them, nothing could stop them from destroying her other children: for she had also created vampires and werewolves, rougarous, and wendigos, and she loved all of her children equally. She knew once the dragons left the darkness, it was only a matter of time before they obliterated all creatures, including themselves. So Hypolyes made the ultimate sacrifice for his Mother and fell upon his own blade. Legend says the Mother wept as she filled a pitcher with his blood, but she knew the sacrifice of one of her children would save the lives of many more. Five swords were forged from this blood and scattered across the earth. When the dragons began their uprising, they were so astounded to discover that there was a weapon powerful enough to slay them that they retreated to their caves and dark places once more. No one saw a dragon for centuries, and the swords became lost, the memories of dragon-fire became legend.

But the swords still exist, and the dragon-fire still burns. The time will come when they will come out of the darkness once more.

NAMES

DEAR DIARY,

I know, this is getting ridiculous, right? Bits and pieces of memory are floating in front of my eyes, but I've lost the context. Don't know what they really mean. Just now, I had this vision of a piece of paper full'a names. I've got no idea where it came from or when I saw it. Could they be hunters? There's no last names, no phone numbers, no nothing. Just names. It *must* be important, right? They wouldn't be swimming around my subconscious if they weren't, but . . . I don't know. Here they are:

George
Daniel
Stephen
Edward (my dad's name, I think.
   I can't even remember.)
Matthew

These have got to mean something. It feels like it's right on the tip of my tongue, but I can't work it out. Maybe it was a list of victims from some monster hunt I went on. Maybe they're the names of all the innocent people that got killed because I wasn't good enough at my job. Maybe it's all meaningless.

Timothy
Chester
Isaac (I think that was Karen's dad's name)

Some women's names as well:

Maria
Sarah
Carolyn
Madeline
Rose
Josephine

. . . . .

Dammit. I realized what this was. Personal. Just . . . don't worry about it.

Now back to our regularly scheduled programming.

OMAHA

CAN'T AVOID IT ANY LONGER. I feel like my whole life is shattering, like things I did when I was a kid are getting confused with things I did last week. I was on a Boy Scout camping trip and hunted a skinwalker. No, that's . . . that doesn't make any sense. I have to write down the things that still *do* make sense.

Omaha. I was in Omaha with Rufus, and we were on the trail of something fierce. We had been together long enough to know what we were capable of, and what we'd need help with, and this was one where we needed backup.

We called the usual suspects: John Winchester, Martin Creaser, Daniel Elkins, but none of 'em could make it in time. The thing we were chasing had killed fourteen people in five days. Or was it four people in two days? I'm missing pieces here. I'm missing huge *chunks*, really. All I know is, if we didn't go after the thing right there and then people were gonna die, and their blood would be on our hands.

I'm proud of what I do. Of helping people, of

trying to make the world better and safer and less . . . evil. But I'm not proud of what I did next.

I called Rufus's daughter. She'd grown into an independent young woman, and since she already knew about the work we did, I didn't see the harm in asking if she could help us out for a day. I wasn't asking her to hunt anything. I wasn't asking her to hold or fire a gun, or put herself in the line of fire, all we needed was a lookout. Or . . . a driver? I know I wouldn't have put her in danger. I couldn't, because I knew she was all Rufus had. He and his mostly off-again girlfriend were never going to be soul mates, they were never going to grow old together. His daughter, though, she was with him through everything. He'd call her every day from the road, tell her what he'd seen. Confide in her in ways I was envious of . . . I guess that's why I'm saying all this now.

When the time came for us to make our move, she was there. I didn't have time to tell Rufus beforehand, and he was furious. Almost walked away from the whole thing, but . . .

Did he walk away?

Or am I just getting this all backwards?

At the end of the day, Rufus and I had killed our prey, but not before it had killed his daughter. An innocent bystander, caught in the middle of a situation she never should have been in.

After that, Rufus went his own way. I went back to Sioux Falls, into a self-imposed exile for a while. Didn't feel like I had any business trying to protect people if I couldn't even protect my partner's kid. That was the last time I was regularly on the road. Ever since, I've thought of myself as more of a command post for hunters, a resource to call on. I put myself into dishonorable retirement. I was thankful the *hantaa* couldn't see what I'd become.

I got her killed. I made the world a lot worse that day.

THE DEPARTED

I'VE LOST SO MANY FRIENDS over the years. Probably the only reason it hasn't driven me completely crazy (before now, I guess, since most people would define not remembering half your life as crazy) is because I don't let myself think about it. There's something really sad about being the last of a generation. Almost everyone I came up with is dead. I'm the oldest hunter I know. I'm the only one who remembers the old way of doing things, before the Internet and Facebook and sexting. Samuel Campbell, Sam and Dean's grandfather who was brought back from the dead for too-complicated-to-explain reasons, he was like me. Couldn't tell a USB port from a hole in the ground. Like we were cut from the same cloth, except I'm me and he was a total friggin' bastard. And now he's dead, for the second time. See how it goes?

Karen. Said about all I can say about her. Still miss her every day.

John Winchester. I had plenty of issues with the

man, mostly how he treated his kids like just another set of duffel bags to drag with him from hunt to hunt, but know this: John was as good a hunter as there ever was, and one of those fundamentally decent guys who you knew would never stab you in the back. Didn't stop me from firing off some rock-salt at him the last time I saw him, but what's a spot of gun violence among friends? I'd give anything to get John back, if only for Sam and Dean. Those boys have lost so much in their lives, losing their dad was just the terrible icing on the horrible cake.

Ellen, Bill, and Jo Harvelle. I never got to know Bill all that well, but John was pretty close with him. They would go on hunts together every now and then, when one of 'em felt like they needed some more horsepower. That story ended in total tragedy—Bill was on a hunt with John when he got killed, and Ellen never forgave John for it. Bill had a kid, Jo, and that girl needed her father.

Maybe things woulda gone differently for Jo if her dad had lived. I'd like to think that he'd never let her take up hunting, no matter how bad she wanted to follow in his footsteps. It's a job for people who have no other choice, and that girl was so bright, she had so many other places her life coulda gone. I know Ellen blamed Sam and Dean a little bit for Jo taking up the rock-salt shotgun, but it wasn't really their fault. They just did what they did, and she wanted to be part of it. It was her daddy—he shouldn't have exposed her to it. What was he thinking? Letting a little girl learn about all the terrible things that are out there prowling the dark, that's what a dad's supposed to *protect* his kids from. Boys *and* girls.

Jo wanted to be a hunter so bad it killed her. I . . . I know, after what I just told you about Rufus and his daughter, I'm not one to talk. That's why I feel so bad about Jo. I thought I'd learned that damn lesson, but I didn't. It took two kids dying for me to see it. *If you have kids, retire.* They need you more than the world does.

Ellen, she was a piece of work. I mean that in the best possible way. The woman was tough as nails, but still sweet as a cup of sugar. When she died (her and Jo, they sacrificed themselves to give Sam and Dean a shot at taking out Lucifer, only for the boys' plan to fail), I wasn't right for weeks. Some things just ain't fair, and that was one of them. We're the good guys. We're supposed to come out on top. That's how it is in movies, that's how it should be in the real world, but I've seen enough heroes get torn apart to know that there are times when the bad guys win. The end of *The Empire Strikes Back*, you know, that's the truth. That's the world. It can't be *Return of the Jedi* all the time. Am I even making sense anymore? Ellen and I were the last of a generation, and now she's gone. Martin Creaser don't count, he's loony as a . . . a loon. God, I can't even put together a sentence anymore.

Rufus Turner. Already told you about most of my time with Rufus, and about our falling out, but I didn't tell you how he died. Last few months, we've been wrapped up in this purgatory business. See, purgatory is like heaven or hell, sort of an alternate plane of existence, parallel to our own, but where heaven is filled with the souls of the righteous and hell is filled with jerk-offs, murderers, and people who talk at the movies, purgatory is full'a monsters. I guess in purgatory they're not considered monsters, but whatever. When a critter dies (vamp, rougarou, whatever) their souls don't go up or down, they go sideways. Souls, since they're incredibly powerful, are like celestial ammunition. Heaven and hell both want 'em so they can keep waging their pissing match for the fate of earth. If heaven or hell could get their mitts on the souls in purgatory, they could turn the tide of their war, maybe even end it for good. The powers that be in hell made an attempt at cracking open purgatory, which pissed off the shrew in charge there—the gal who created all the monsters in the first place, who they call "the Mother of All," or Eve. Eve came through to earth and . . . she wasn't pleased with us hunters for killing so many of her children over the years. She set a trap for us and turned us against each other. In the chaos, Rufus was stabbed. I tried to tell him that I was sorry for what happened in Omaha, but he wouldn't let me. He went to his grave holding that against me . . . *wanting* to hate me for it. I guess he had the right. I hope he rests in peace.

Adam Milligan. Sam and Dean's half-brother, he got the short end of the stick for sure. Before they even met him, Adam was already dead, killed by ghouls.

When Dean wouldn't say yes to Michael during the Apocalypse, Michael ordered Zachariah to raise Adam from the dead. He was brought back to life just to be a pawn in a game of celestial chicken—Michael had no intention of using Adam as a vessel, he just wanted to provoke a reaction from Dean. When Dean *still* said no to Michael, he reluctantly took Adam as a vessel instead, and Adam ended up trapped in hell with Michael and Satan. The torment that boy must be going through, I can't even imagine.

Ash. A genius, though you'd never know by looking at him. He died when the Harvelle's roadhouse was burned down. Gone way too young, like Jo.

Pamela Barnes. Why do the good-looking ones always have to die?

R. C. Adams, Jed Thurnby, Carl Moore, Olivia Lowry. All killed by the Rising of the Witnesses. As if hunters needed any more guilt about the people they didn't save.

Isaac Foster. Killed by the demon Gluttony. His kid was killed by a demon, that's how he and Tamara, his wife, got into hunting. Hopefully he's with his daughter now. Hopefully he thinks it was all worth it.

Daniel Elkins. The man who was credited with hunting vampires to extinction, killed by vampires. Ironic way to go, but he wouldn't have it any other way. He told me on more than one occasion that he knew he'd go down bloody, and he was right.

Caleb Johnson. Killed by Meg Masters. Never

knew him as well as I should have, but he was a damn good hunter.

And then there's the whole Campbell Clan—Samuel, Mark, Gwen, Christian, a few more. A year ago, I didn't know any of them. They came into my life and exited it just as fast—every single one of them is dead. A whole hunter legacy, destroyed. As far as I know, Sam and Dean are the end of the line . . . and I don't see them having kids anytime soon, if ever. Because if they did, I hope they'd know better than to keep hunting.

Something tells me both of the Winchester boys will still be hunting when their names get added to this list, and that that day will come too soon.

FRIED FOODS

GOD, I'M FALLING APART NOW. Everything's disappearing. What else do I need to remember?

Okay. This might not seem important, but it is to me. My favorite fried foods:

- **Chicken-fried bacon.** It exists. Got it at the Lincoln County Fair, four years back. The same day I met a lady named Reba, fell in love with her, head over steel-toed boots, woulda married her . . . then woke up the next morning and couldn't stand the woman. *That* is how good chicken-fried bacon is. I'd highly recommend you do whatever you've gotta do to get your hands on some of this before you die, because otherwise your life just ain't complete.

- **Fried Twinkies.** Do I need to explain this? Moving on.

- **Deep-fried beer.** This one's rare, not just anybody can make it happen, but when they do . . . heaven. I mean that literally. When I'm up in heaven, you can bet your ass that this is what I'll be eating. Plus, it's an upper and a downer. Fried food raises your blood pressure, the beer relaxes you. Balances itself right out. Science.

- **Deep-fried turkey.** Wouldn't be Thanksgiving without it. When I was a kid, it wouldn't be Thanksgiving without one of my uncles getting drunk and crashing his four-wheeler into our neighbor's chicken coop. That way, you get both turkey *and* chicken for dinner, 'cause my old man would have to pay for the dead chickens, and we didn't waste food just because it had tire tread marks on it.

- **Fried pizza.** Simpler than you'd think. Place in Sheboygan does it, could kill a man just breathing the oily air in that hole. That said, I'd never pass up a chance to eat something that's greasy on the outside *and* the inside.

- **Flautas.** I chased a wendigo across the Mexican border back in '94, ended up staying a month. There was this little cafe, nothing more than a neon sign in a woman's living room window . . . best food I ever ate. Place didn't even have a name, just the neon sign, which said "Flautas." I'm telling you, you'd kill a man to get your hands on these little tubes of fried joy. The hostess wasn't hard to look at, either. I'd tell you to look it up if you're ever in those parts, but last I heard the whole town was wiped out in a mudslide—during the Apocalypse. Thanks a lot, Satan . . . ya jag.

LAST WILL AND TESTAMENT

I DON'T HAVE MUCH in the way of property, but I think the time's come to say where I want it all to go once I'm gone.

My collection of cars, though they're in rough shape, goes to Dean Winchester. Treat them half as well as you treat the Impala, and they'll be in better hands than they ever were with me.

My guns, those go to Sam. Because I don't want you to feel left out, mostly, and I know you'll share with Dean. My real gift to you, Sam, is giving you permission to digitize all my books, like you've been bugging me to do for years. Have fun with it.

My house, burn to the damn ground. This place still holds so many terrible memories for me, it's a wonder I've been able to live here myself. Let someone else start here fresh, with a new home that won't have all this baggage.

My books, those go to hunters everywhere. Do

what you have to do to get them out into the world, to where they can actually help people.

Everything else, give to charity. To folks who are down on their luck, in the same way that I've been, so many times.

. . . . .

I'm going to try to close my eyes for a bit. I hope I wake up.

SAM AND DEAN

WHOA. Something just . . . *snapped* in my brain. I saw that woman, from the bog, but this time she was against a field of stars . . . but not outside. They were stars *painted* on something. Where was she?

I hoped this mental exercise would help dislodge a memory, that I'd remember some clue that could help me fix myself, but . . . I'm no better off now than I was when I started. Worse, really, since most of my mind is gone. It's like . . . something is *searching* my memory, and throwing out the bits they don't want. As for what that thing might be, I've gone through every possibility I know of, written it all down, but I've failed.

The thought has occurred to me that whatever it is, it could be in my house. It could be right here, laughing at me from the shadows as I flail around, trying to stop the inevitable. Damn. I guess I really think that . . . it *is* inevitable.

I don't say this often, but I'm giving up.

Said everything I need to say, left what instructions I can remember. I could go on for a thousand pages more, but that's what my library's for. If you need answers you can't find here, you know where to look. Or call Sam and Dean, or Creaser, or Visyak, Rodger Stanton, or Willie Freeman—their numbers are . . . somewhere. I don't even know where I keep them any more.

So that's it. I'm ending this little *memento mori* with a final note. A message for Sam and Dean, if they ever find this.

I first met Sam and Dean when they were tiny. Dean must have been six or seven, Sam three. Even then, you could see their personalities clear as day. Dean was daddy's good little soldier, walking and talking like John as best he could, while Sam was quieter—more reserved, introspective, looking at the world and really thinking about it before he acted. I never knew Mary, but I imagine that's how she was, too.

By the time I really got to know the Winchester family, I'd already given up the road life and settled back into Sioux Falls. John would call me often enough to ask for intel, backup, or a place to crash. Most often, though, he'd need a place to drop the boys while he went after some dangerous thing.

To them, I was Uncle Bobby—the old kook with the really cool backyard. Even Sam, who wasn't much into cars, couldn't help but have fun back in the salvage yard, playing hide and seek with Dean and imagining the stories behind each one of the cars. Did it have a family? Did they miss it?

When John would come back from his hunts, we'd all sit around my kitchen table and talk about what'd happened while he was gone. John would make up some story about his sales job for Sam's benefit, which Dean saw right through. Sam would sit and listen, sometimes tell John about a book he'd read while John was gone. When Sam had gone to bed, Dean would rattle off all the lore he'd learned from poking through my library, so proud to be one of the men.

Then, they'd disappear for a few months. I worried so much for those boys, it was like seeing my own sons go off to war each time they drove away. John was a great hunter, but he wasn't careful. Not careful enough, anyway, to have two small kids with him.

In 1991, I gave Sam a present to give John for Christmas. It was an amulet that I got in trade from a woman in Tampa who said it was a protective charm. My intention was dead simple—if I could do anything to make sure John was always there for his boys, I'd do it. The next time I saw them, in January of '92, Dean was wearing the amulet. Sam had given it to him instead, and I asked why. Sam had learned the truth about what John did, and the risks he took every day. Sam felt betrayed that John had lied to him for so long. It didn't make sense to him that his dad would go so far out of his way and risk so much for other people instead of protecting his own kids.

That was the true beginning of Sam's falling out with John, and I have to say . . . I agreed with Sam.

At the same time, I'd lost my own wife to a demon. I never got my revenge. I understood John. But . . . when Karen died, I was left with nothing. *John had a family.* He had so much left to live for, I was envious of him. If those'd been my boys, no way I woulda gone after the demon that killed their mom. I woulda plopped 'em down in a nice town, tried to make sure their lives were as normal as I could.

I know, that's all talk. I wasn't in John's shoes, I can't truly know what I woulda done. But John's quest for vengeance killed him and dragged his sons into a life that'll eventually kill them too (it already has a few times, but so far it hasn't stuck).

One day, the Winchesters showed up on my doorstep and Dean had a gun in his belt. He was twelve years old. I'd known that the boys knew how to shoot—hell, I'd taken them out back for target practice myself, but that was too far. I tried to talk to John about it, but he wouldn't hear it. "They need to know the truth about what's out there, Bobby," he said to me. "I need to make sure they're ready."

He trained those boys like they were Navy SEALs. Dean was more excited about it, but Sam was a good shot, too. They were well versed in all kinds of monster lore, they knew the difference between a ghost and a poltergeist (a poltergeist can move stuff), they could field strip a rifle in thirty seconds. They also never really got a chance to be kids.

John left them with me to go on a hunting trip to Montana, said he would be gone a week. After ten days, I started to get worried. He had a cell phone by that point, but he wasn't answering it. The boys were old enough to tell I was worried, but I played it off. Told them that I'd spoken to John, and that he'd be back for them as soon as he could. Secretly, I started calling hospitals and morgues all over Montana, seeing if his body had turned up somewhere.

After two weeks, I started calling every hunter I

knew, to see if anybody could go up there to check in on him. I couldn't leave the boys alone, that'd make me as bad as John. Nobody was available—the nineties were busy years for hunters. All I could do was keep waiting.

It was summer, so the boys weren't in school. I did my best to keep them occupied, to keep them from asking too many questions about where John was and when he was coming back. Sam was the worst, since he was littler and still naive. He'd believe any lie I told him, but it killed me to do it.

After a month, I accepted the fact that John was dead. Figuring out how to tell Sam and Dean was one of the hardest things I've ever had to do, and I hated John for making me do it. I sat them down in my living room, but couldn't even bring myself to say the words. I had tears in my eyes when I finally said it. "Boys, your dad's not coming back this time."

Sam was so in shock, he couldn't even cry. Dean, he screamed at me. Called me a liar, told me that John was too tough to die, that he was just busy with a case, and he'd be home soon. I wanted to say, "You're right, Dean. I'm sure he'll be back soon." I couldn't. I had to tear the bandage off, make Dean understand that holding out hope for John's return would only make things worse. Dean and I have never argued that bad since. He was screaming, pounding on my chest, cursing me out for not having any faith in John. All the while, Sam just sat there, silent. Taking it all in.

I went too far. In trying to make Dean understand, I said things about John I couldn't take back. Things that no son should ever hear about his father. I said John was an idiot, a damn fool for chasing the thing that'd killed their mom, and that they'd be better off having been put in an orphanage after Mary died rather than being dragged around by John. Every bad thought I'd ever had about him, I let out right then and there. Between that and what happened in Omaha, I've told you the two moments I'm least proud of.

Dean stormed off, disappeared into the forest by my house. For ten hours I waited for him to come back. As I contemplated having to call the police to help find him, I realized just how much Dean was like his dad. And that Dean's reaction was just his way of processing what he must have known to be true—that John really wasn't coming back. I'd made things so much worse than they needed to be. And poor Sam . . . smart enough to know exactly what was happening, but shy enough to bear it all in silence. God only knows the pain he was feeling.

At midnight, I heard footsteps on my front steps. When I opened the door, there was Dean, holding John Winchester's hand.

He was alive. And when he returned, he found his son on the side of the highway, trying to hitch a ride to Montana to look for him.

When John saw me, there was ice in his eyes. He was so furious at me for what I'd said to Dean and Sam, he coulda sucker-punched me. He called out for

Sam, who was asleep on the couch. Said they were leaving, going to stay with some *real* friends.

I told you I wasn't proud of what I said to Dean, but I'm also not that proud of what I did next—I grabbed a rock-salt shotgun from my shelf and chased John off my property, blasting the back of the Impala with salt as it skidded out of my driveway.

I spent the next few years regretting what'd happened. Hunting can be a lonely life, and it was a lot lonelier without the Winchesters. I may put on a gruff exterior, but everybody wants a family. That's what John had, and I felt like he was throwing it away.

The next time I saw Dean and Sam, it was years later, and they were grown. Sam had gone to college, Dean had started hunting solo. They'd joined up to find John, who'd (again) gone missing. It was the same old story, except this time they were both old enough to know the truth about John.

They eventually found him, but their reunion didn't last. John gave up his life to save Dean's, and was sent to hell for his trouble. Sam, Dean, and I were able to open the Devil's Gate in Wyoming and let him out, and finally get vengeance on the Yellow-eyed Demon for what the bastard did to Mary Winchester.

Having the boys back in my life has been one of the best things that's ever happened to me. Felt like it gave me a purpose I hadn't had in years. Gave me a family again.

If I've taken anything from my life, it's this—you choose your family. It's not just blood, it's not just the cards you're dealt, life is about what you make for yourself, who you choose to spend your days with. If Sam and Dean are what I've made for myself, then I feel like I've done damn good.

I'm trying to remember the last time I saw their faces. Ashland is a blur. Must have been a couple weeks before that. Dean made Sam drop everything for an AC/DC show in Rapid City, and I made the trip out to meet them. Dean pushed his way into the crowd at the amphitheater, came back out bloody—no. That wasn't Rapid City. Where was it? Dean, his face bloody, like he'd been beaten within an inch of his life.

That was Ashland.

The stars were behind him, too. Painted stars.

The Starry Nite Inn, off Highway 13, two miles outside of Ashland. That's where Sam and Dean were staying. That's where the woman took us, after the bog.

I'm leaving, right now. Gonna go back there, try to find them, try to find that woman I keep seeing . . . and if she's what did this to me, I'm gonna kill her.

I hope I never have to finish this journal. If you find this text and I'm dead, spread the word. Keep fighting the good fight.

— *Bobby Singer, 2011*

OBLIVION

UH. HI.

I'm not Bobby.

My name is Dean Winchester, and I'm not quite
sure how to explain what's happened the last few
days. Guess with these things you start at the beginning. I'm no writer, so bear with me.

My brother Sam and I were in northern Wisconsin, chasing down a lead on something that'd disappeared a few dudes. My money was on a succubus or
siren, but Sammy bet crocotta. That's when we got
the call about an Eve sighting in Port Washington,
a few hours south. Eve was a big fish (not, you know,
literally), so we had to jump off the Ashland case and
called in Bobby to take over for us. Shocking nobody,
he was a grumperpuss about it, but got in that beat
up old Chevelle of his and drove up.

When we came back from Port Washington (the
Eve thing was a false alarm), Bobby'd done most of
the legwork for us. It turned out to be a banshee we
were after, so Sammy and I were both wrong. In his

infinite wisdom, Bobby'd gotten the banshee hooked on *him*, so we were looking at a countdown situation. Sooner or later, Bobby would fly the belfry and disappear on us, so we had to stay with him wherever he went. And boy, Bobby's a regular Chatty Cathy when you're with him all day.

He started getting antsy, wanted to go to the bog real bad, so the banshee's call had definitely kicked in. Before we drove to the swamp, Bobby had to sing this terrible song into Sam's phone, said it was the only way to off the banshee, and hey, he was the expert. Felt like we were the ones getting punished, though.

Bobby already told you how things went with the banshee. She wasn't the problem. This other— pardon my French—*total bitch* came out of nowhere and beat the living crap out of us and we all woke up back in our hotel, the Starry Nite Inn on Highway 13.

The woman was standing over Bobby, working some bad-touch mojo on him. His face was all twisted up in pain, like he'd eaten some bad shellfish or something. She was talking to him, whispering, too low for me to hear.

Sam and I were tied to chairs, which happens to us so often that we oughta hide knives in our sleeves. Being absolute geniuses, though, we don't do that. Maybe we'll start, right after we put our weapons on a bungee. I could tell Sam was already working on his bindings, and so was I, but it'd take us a minute.

The woman touched her finger to Bobby's temple, did some kinda Vulcan mind meld on him, and when she took her finger away, a trail of white light followed, like she was tugging out a string of pure energy. Whatever she was doing, Bobby did not seem jazzed about it. She took her finger, dragging the white light with it, and touched her own temple. Like she was making a psychic connection between them.

There wasn't anything we could do except watch and make angry faces at the lady. Bobby started mumbling, babbling nonsense, like he didn't know where he was. The bitch was messing with his mind, putting a tap into his brain and letting all the juice drip out.

Sam, being Sam, got out of his binds first. Those huge biceps aren't just for impressing other dudes at the gym. The woman raised her hand, clenched her fist, and he was sent flying ass-over-elbows, knocked right into me. My chair tipped backwards, which actually helped me out, since it put me in a better position to get at the knot in my rope. I was up a few seconds later and saw Sam get his ass handed to him a second time. Guy is always getting beat up by girls.

When I went at her, I won't say it went great, but I didn't get flung into a wall. She might have punched me a little, but I got in a few blows, too. Sam came in behind her and got a hand around her neck, while I went for the pillow on the bed, where I'd stashed a knife and a gun.

That's when things got weird.

Bobby stood up, started going crazy. And I mean *cuh-ray-zee*. Taking swings at all of us, demanding we take him to the bus stop, crap like that. She must have really scrambled his eggs, because a second later he ran out of the room and didn't look back. Last I saw him, his Chevelle was fish-tailing out of the Starry Nite's parking lot.

And then the lady *really* got pissed off.

. . . . .

I don't like getting my ass kicked any more than the next guy, but it's a little more embarrassing when your job is to kick other people's asses. Anyway, the next few days weren't exactly the champagne room at the Spearmint Rhino. Sam and I were kept in that hotel room and got our noodles twirled, just like Bobby did.

Parts of my memory are fuzzy (because of the noodle twirling . . . , but it felt like she was scanning my brain. Sampling what she found inside, and psychically ripping out the parts that she liked. Every now and then, she'd laugh, cry, or start talking to herself, reliving the memories she was taking from us. As she took the memories, they'd flash in our heads. Little pieces of them, like echoes.

She was still taking memories from Bobby, too. Once she put that tap in his brain, she was able to siphon off his memories wherever he went. Pretty good racket, I guess, if stealing other people's lives is your thing. What she was doing with the memories and why she picked the ones she picked, she kept that to herself.

While I was tied up, having my grapefruit juiced, I got to thinking. That after what she'd done to him, maybe I'd never see Bobby again. He didn't seem to be in any shape to come rescue us, and the guy was the only person who knew we were here.

I shouldn't have doubted him.

It took him a few days, but Bobby showed. While the lady was forcing me to relive the tenth grade, Bobby smashed through the hotel room door. He blasted her with rock-salt before she'd even turned around. Black blood sprayed on the tacky star wallpaper—kind of an improvement, really. Didn't drop the shrew, though, she came right back at him. Another shell straight to her gut and she doubled over. Bobby got to Sammy first, untied him, then came for me.

Three on one, it was a pretty even fight. We had her cornered, Bobby pulled a silver knife from his jacket, took a couple swipes, then fell over, having a seizure. Then Sammy fell over, too. When Sam looked up at me, it was like he didn't even recognize me. A blank stare.

My whole life flashed through my head—every kick, every kiss, every monster, and every bacon cheeseburger. All of them felt totally real, as if I was experiencing every flavor I ever tasted at the same time. And man, they tasted funny together.

I had to fight through it to get back on my feet. The woman was straining, holding out her hands at me and Sammy. Bobby was back on his feet as well, struggling to move towards her. I fell back to the floor, totally useless. Imagine feeling every emotion you've ever felt, simultaneously. I didn't know whether to cry, laugh, or puke, but I came close to doing all three. When I looked back up, Bobby had his knife to her neck. She was talking, but all I could hear were the voices in my head—my dad's voice, Sam's voice, my *mom's* voice, telling me that angels were watching over me. . . .

It stopped fast, like a faucet was turned off. I wiped the tears off my cheeks in the manliest way possible, then saw that she and Bobby were still facing off. His knife and her hand both raised.

"Who are you?" he asked.

She smiled at him, in that totally creepy way that monsters do. "Oblivion. Lethe. The Great River," she said back, and this is verbatim 'cause I couldn't make this crap up.

Bobby shook his head. "Not familiar."

You know what else is chatty, besides Bobby? Monsters. They love to tell you their story and blather on about how terrible their lives are, what a burden they bear, yada yada yada. This one was no different.

See, Oblivion, aka Lethe, aka crazy shrew, was a high-level goddess in Greek mythology. Her job? Wiping people's memories, which, I know, is a huge shock. She liked her job and was apparently really good at it. She dug the, I don't know, *taste* of the memories she'd take.

Bobby has a picture of her in one of his books, but it don't do her justice:

Oblivion got her orders from the men upstairs, and it'd worked that way since Adam and Eve were playing "hide the kielbasa" in the Garden of Eden. People see things they're not supposed to see every day, and she was the one who would swoop in and remove those memories. Like a celestial housekeeper.

Except a recession had hit in heaven, and she was laid off. We'd averted the Apocalypse, and the great heavenly plan had been tossed out. Just like the Fates, Oblivion's services were no longer needed. Team Free Will, baby.

But Oblivion, she enjoyed her job too much to give it up. Like one of those accountants who retires but still does people's taxes for fun. There was no order from heaven for her to take our memories. No plan. She said if angels like Balthazar could run around doing whatever the hell they wanted, then she was gonna do the same thing.

Bobby asked her what she wanted from us, and she told him the honest truth. One memory, that's all. One of *Bobby's* memories. She could smell it from across the state, and used the banshee as a way to lure us in. Sammy and me, we were just collateral damage.

I asked what was wrong with my memories. I mean, what am I, chopped liver? What she said will stay with me for the rest of my life. She said she'd sampled all of our goods, and even with everything me and Sam had been through, Bobby'd still had it worse. He'd been forced to kill his own wife, twice, and bury nearly every friend he'd ever had. He'd seen enough terrible things for a hundred lifetimes. And despite all that baggage, deep inside him, he was hiding a single, perfect memory. A moment of . . . bliss, I guess. *That* is what she wanted. That flawless moment.

But it was hidden too well for her to find. She'd been trying to draw it out, but it was under layers of pure suffering that she couldn't get through. That's why she needed him to come back to Ashland, and why she'd been using her psychic connection to Bobby to send him clues—images of her, of me, of what went down with the banshee, returning just enough of his memories so that he'd find his way back to her. She wanted to bargain.

That one memory for all of our lives. Knowing Bobby, I thought he'd say yes right away. Never met someone so prone to self-sacrifice. But I hoped he wouldn't. He had something in there that was rare, like one in a million, she said. If I had that, I'd keep it hidden, too. But if he refused her offer, she'd suck out what she could from our heads and leave us to die as vegetables.

Bobby, bless his surly heart, said no. Told her to eat a bag of dicks. Said he was through making deals with the likes of her. He knew exactly what memory she was talking about, and he'd rather die than give it up. He was being a little cavalier with me and Sam's lives, but I dug his attitude.

Oblivion knew his blind spot, though. Karen. Apparently, Bobby'd realized he was losing his memories while he was driving home to Sioux Falls. He was so scared of losing his memories of Karen that he carved her name in his car's windshield at a rest stop along the way. Oblivion watched through her psychic connection as Bobby wrote down the story of her death and saw that set him on his path to being a hunter. If he cared for her so much, how would he feel if she never knew he existed? Oblivion had a pass-card for the pearly gates of heaven. Some of the people she wiped were *already dead*—in Greek mythology, the river Lethe was where souls went to be wiped clean before they were reincarnated—so she could find Karen in heaven and steal all of her memories of Bobby. If they ever got to meet again, Bobby'd still love her, but she wouldn't even know his name.

"So, what'll it be?" she said. "Will you give up the memory for Karen?"

To Bobby, it wasn't even a choice. He said yes.

. . . . .

Oblivion put her hands on Bobby's face. He was sitting in a chair, she stood over him. Once she had the memory, she'd let us go, she said. I've met enough monsters to know that once they've tasted the chum in the water, they never let you go. She'd take Bobby's perfect memory, then the rest of him, then me, then Sam. We had to fight back.

Bobby said he was ready, leaned back in the chair. Closed his eyes, concentrating. It was time to do . . . something.

Sometimes, when I'm in a really stressful situation, I think of this hilarious picture of Sammy from when he was two years old. He's buck naked and playing air guitar to Zeppelin's "Kashmir." That was before he decided to hate good music. I have no idea why it always pops into my head, but it takes the edge off. I was about to watch my friend get lobotomized, and what do you know, there was Sammy, riffing on his air guitar.

The damnedest thing happened. Oblivion *laughed*.

The connection between us was still active. Everything I remembered, *she remembered*. Finally, I had a weapon.

I pictured Alastair, branding me with a scorching hot piece of iron. Rusty hooks, being driven through my skin. Boiling water, being poured down my throat.

Oblivion flinched, pulled away from Bobby. Confused.

A scalpel, zippering open the flesh on my chest. A nail, being driven through my hands. A needle, digging into my eye. It was hell, literally. I was reliving my time in hell.

Oblivion snarled, wracked with pain.

"Sam, use hell," I said. "Think about hell." He only remembered a few seconds of his time in the Pit, but it was with Lucifer himself—a few seconds was more than enough.

Sam nodded, concentrated—I was worried he'd have a seizure, like he did the last time he remembered his time in hell, but that'd be better than us all getting our brains sucked out.

Oblivion reached her hand out at me, but I just kept thinking about hell. Picturing years worth of torture, at the hands of a demon who knew what he was doing.

Then, my mother. Mary Winchester, smiling at me. Oblivion was putting the image in my head, and I had to fight it. I had to replace it with something terrible.

Bobby stood, one of Oblivion's hands still on his face. Grabbed her hand.

I thought about losing my dad. Getting torn up by the hellhounds. Watching Sam die by Jake's hand.

A knife. Bobby had a knife in his hand. Oblivion screamed.

I watched the fire burning down our house in Lawrence. Burning up my mom's body. I watched Sam fall into hell.

A flash of silver. Bobby stabbed the knife into Oblivion's chest. She fell back, a burst of white light flying out of her mouth. Into me, into Sam, into Bobby, and a thousand more directions. Our memories, put back right where she took them from.

We were all quiet for a second. Not sure if that'd really just happened. Then Bobby went to our duffel bag, pulled out a machete. Started hacking into Oblivion's body.

I asked him what he was doing.

He smiled at me, like he was remembering something hilarious. He said, "It ain't dead till it's in five pieces."

THE HIDDEN MEMORY

HEY, DEAN AGAIN. I owe you some more explanations.

We're all back in Sioux Falls, now, looking for our next case. I found this stack of papers in the trash, read through them. Had no idea Bobby'd been through so much, or how close we all came to losing on this one.

Bobby didn't want to finish this book. Said he didn't have anything else to add. I told him that it was too important to throw away. Some day, we'll all get put in the ground, and somebody is gonna need to pick things up where we left off. That he owed it to himself to put an ending on this story, to leave something behind. He told me to do it myself, so here we are.

I told you what happened with Oblivion. But there's a missing piece. After we bailed on the Starry Night Inn, I asked Bobby about the memory. What it was that Oblivion wanted so bad. He just harumphed and got in his van, drove off.

There are clues, though. You read what he wrote,

right? The man is a curmudgeon on the outside, but downright obsessed with family. That's why he was always tough on my old man, because my dad had what Bobby wanted—kids.

Then there's the list of names, couple chapters back. Made me think—what if those were the names he was gonna use for his kids, if he ever had them?

I think Bobby's been holding on to a memory for years, one that tears him up inside, but is too important to let go of. Hear me out on this—I *think that Bobby was going to be a father*. That Karen was pregnant when she died, and the memory he's been carting around, it's of her telling him. I have no way to prove it, but there it is. She told Bobby he was going to be a dad, and a few weeks later he had to kill her. A perfect memory, surrounded by misery, grief, and regret. Maybe his *last* good memory of Karen, the one love of his life.

But, end of the day, it's Bobby's memory. The good thing about memories is that they're private. Can't be taken or traded or stolen (most of the time). So I'm done asking about it. If he ever wants to share, he knows my number.

Me and Bobby, we've spent the last few days rebuilding his Chevelle. He did the same for me when the Impala was busted up, I figured I owed him one. It's . . . it kind of reminds me of working with my dad. If Bobby *did* lose a kid, and I lost a father, well . . . then maybe what we've got ain't a bad substitute. Bobby's right. Family isn't just blood.

ABOUT THE AUTHOR

DAVID REED works as the script coordinator on *Super-natural* and wrote the stories for the episodes "Hammer of the Gods" and "You Can't Handle the Truth," along with several TV movies and comic books. In his spare time (ha!) he likes to hang out with his wife and son, who are pretty great. He can often be found in front of the television with a death grip on an Xbox 360 controller, or at the L.A. zoo, making animal sounds with (and at) his toddler.

COMPLETE YOUR
SUPERNATURAL™
LIBRARY

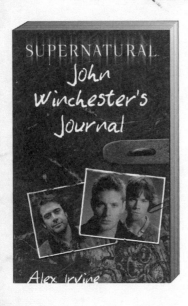

SUPERNATURAL
John Winchester's
Journal

In John's personal journal, he compiled folklore, legend, superstition, and his own experiences with otherworldly enemies.

The SUPERNATURAL Book
of Monsters, Demons,
Spirits and Ghouls

Here is an indispensable guide to the otherworldly creatures seen on the series, with annotations by Sam, Dean, and their father.

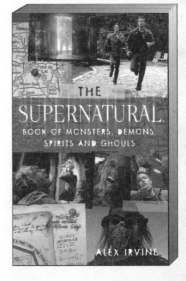

itbooks
AN IMPRINT OF HARPERCOLLINS PUBLISHERS

Available wherever books are sold.

SUPERNATURAL™ & © Warner Bros. Entertainment, Inc.